Dying to Meet You

By B. M. Gill

B. M. GILL

Dying to Meet You

A CRIME CLUB BOOK
DOUBLEDAY

New York London Toronto Sydney Auckland

A Crime Club Book
PUBLISHED BY DOUBLEDAY
a division of Bantam Doubleday Dell Publishing Group, Inc.
666 Fifth Avenue, New York, New York 10103

DOUBLEDAY and the portrayal of a man
with a gun are trademarks of Doubleday,
a division of Bantam Doubleday Dell
Publishing Group, Inc.

Library of Congress Cataloging-in-Publication Data

Gill, B. M.
Dying to meet you / B.M. Gill.
p.   cm.
"A Crime Club book."
I.   Title.
PR6057.I538D9   1990
823'.914—dc20   89-25755
CIP

ISBN 0-385-41448-x

Dying to Meet You

ONE

He was strangling Peterson to the accompaniment of Grieg's Piano Concerto in A Minor, Opus 16, third movement. And it wasn't a nightmare. The music from the adjoining showroom was thumping through his head, beating at his heart, pulsating through his fingers as his hands tightened around Peterson's scrawny neck while the words came streaming out of his mouth. And the bastard wouldn't stop talking. The room was black and narrow, constricting his vision so that all he could see was Peterson's mouth opening and closing, opening and closing, like a fish behind glass.

And then the music stopped.

The silence made a physical impression on the room, pushing the walls apart. He began to breathe normally, see normally. Peterson, still seated behind the desk, was looking at him, puzzled.

I could have killed you, Lowell thought, shocked. *Inside my head I was killing you. What is reality? That? Or this?* He helped himself to a tumblerful of water from a carafe on the desk and gulped some of it. There was a chair on the other side of the desk. He hadn't been invited to take it, but he had to sit. On this level, he and Peterson were eye to eye.

Peterson, unaware of how close he had been to sudden

extinction, asked the younger man if he was unwell. Lowell, unable yet to answer, shook his head.

Peterson gave him a few minutes to calm himself and then repeated what he had been saying earlier, but this time with notably less censure in his voice. "I'm not suggesting that you're not trying to give of your best to the job," he hedged. "It's just that you're not clued in to what's expected of you. Let's look at the facts: This is a small company. The pianos we manufacture are not yet household names. They will be in time, but until they are we have to import from Europe—and also from the Far East. Some of the pianos we import are first-class. Out there in the showroom there's a range to suit all tastes, and all pockets. It's your job, Mr. Marshall, to sell them. So if a customer can't afford a top-quality instrument, you don't denigrate what he can afford and lose a sale. Am I being unreasonable in pointing this out?"

Lowell drank more water. The glass was cold on his fingers: the nerve endings were beginning to throb less. He ignored the question.

Peterson raised an eyebrow quizzically, waited, and then continued. "Salesmen are not necessarily born with the gift of selling; they learn the technique. But they need the right motivation, and I don't believe you have it. You're obsessional about your past as a successful concert pianist—you can't accept the fact that your arthritic hands have put an end to it. It's tough. I'm sorry. But other, greater musicians have learnt to live with their disabilities, and so must you." He glanced at a plastic bust of Beethoven on a shelf to the right of the window. "He had his problems, too, as you well know. He couldn't even hear his music."

But I can hear mine, you patronising bastard. All I can produce these days is bloody nursery stuff.

Peterson, not expecting an answer this time, flowed on: "When fate kicks you in the teeth, you're forced to change direction and people, generally speaking, respond sympathetically. When Sir Howard Bentham approached me on your behalf I passed over better applicants."

Buddies at Cambridge, Lowell remembered; that and the masonic handshake. The thought of a handshake—flesh on flesh—was upsetting.

"Your uncle had confidence in your ability to adapt to a new environment and I respected his judgement. But you have been a disappointment to us both." Peterson shook his head sadly. "You must surely see that?"

I see you sitting there mouthing at me, and I daren't look too closely at your smug self-satisfied face or, God help me, it will happen again.

He looked away. The office was opulently furnished in neutral tones, but apart from the bust of Beethoven there was no other obvious link with the music world. On the wall were a couple of original oil paintings—soothing country scenes. It was easier to speak to Peterson if he looked at them.

"This week I lost three sales by being honest about the workmanship of three inferior instruments. I sold one which was worth selling." His voice sounded calmer than he felt. "The one I sold I would be proud to play on, if I were still capable of playing. I told the purchaser it was Lowell Marshall quality—which was a recommendation he wanted to hear. And that was your main reason for taking me on. My name still carries some weight."

Peterson couldn't deny it. Employing this arrogant, haggard-looking, thirty-five-year-old ex-celebrity had been a sales gimmick. Posters showing him on concert platforms in London, Rome and Paris adorned the entrance hall. He hadn't expected him to be a good salesman —and he wasn't. He hadn't expected him to be devastatingly honest to the detriment of the business—but he was.

"Your name will be of decreasing value as time goes on," he said with unintended cruelty. "People forget."

That was true. Most of what Peterson had told him was true. It always was. He had been with the company for eleven months now and today's lecture was one of many. The last of many. Until today he had managed to keep his cool.

He stood up and told Peterson he was resigning. "It's a hasty decision. Give yourself time." Peterson managed to hide his relief. "Why not take your annual leave and think about it?" His response was polite rather than persuasive.

Lowell suggested taking his annual leave in lieu of a month's notice. Starting now.

After a little more prevarication, Peterson agreed. Sir Howard had warned him that his nephew might be troublesome. An awkward cuss. A brilliant musician, thwarted. He'd promised, with a touch of humour, not to withdraw his shares in the company if Peterson sacked him, though sacking wasn't easy in these days of legislation against unfair dismissal. An erosion of confidence—a chipping away at a sensitive ego—had achieved just what he wanted.

By the time Lowell had written and torn up three letters of resignation in the outer office (what the hell did one say? I'm leaving this god awful dump before I kill you?), and then finally produced something terse and acceptable, it was five o'clock. He drove out of the grounds at the same time as the factory workers. They were honest craftsmen and what they produced wasn't bad. He had told the customers it wasn't bad—and that wasn't good enough. In his day he had been an honest performer—according to the music critics, an inspired performer. But this wasn't the music world. This was commerce, and the dichotomy was unacceptable. The violence of his reaction to Peterson, albeit inwardly expressed, appalled him. It had seemed so real. He had believed it was happening.

His shirt was still soaked with sweat and there were patches of damp showing under the armpits of his grey suit. His salesman's grey suit. An obsequious suit with a matching polite tie. He and Zoe had gone out and bought the uniform when she persuaded him to take the job. The opening still had a link with music, she'd pointed out, and there wasn't anything else. Practical Zoe. The money was peanuts compared with what she was earning as a dentist. And her salary had been peanuts compared to what he'd made before his hands packed it in. The see-saw of matrimonial finance had her way up at the moment and his resignation wouldn't make a lot of difference to their income. But even if it had meant total penury he'd still have done the same.

On his way home he called in at the Health Centre, ignored the receptionist, and walked down the corridor to the doctors' surgeries. The evening session had been going about half an hour and there were a couple of elderly women patients waiting outside Ben's door. He told them that he needed to see Dr. Sprackman urgently and when they looked at him they didn't argue. He guessed it was because he looked as awful as he felt.

Ben, surprised to see his neighbour and friend, didn't argue either. He was everything Lowell wasn't. Contented, happy in his marriage, the father of three children. As a general practitioner he coasted along and hoped his few mistakes weren't too terrible. His patients liked and trusted him, while he dealt with their crises with calm efficiency. What, he wondered, was bugging Lowell now?

"I'm sorry for barging in—jumping the queue." Lowell closed the door behind him and leaned up against it. For a moment or two he lacked the energy to walk across the room; his heart was still thumping too fast and his mouth was dry. The surgery wasn't as soothing as he had expected it to be. Since his last professional visit a few months ago it had been redecorated. The original wall-paper had been a pale grey Regency stripe which matched the grey carpet tiles. The carpet tiles were still the same, but the walls now were a bright lemon-and-white trellis. It was disturbing. When you seek a familiar refuge you don't expect to find it all tarted up.

It would have been easier to tell Ben what he had to tell him if the environment hadn't been changed.

He struggled with it. "I've had a kind of black-out—just before coming here—in Peterson's office. He was talking—rubbing my nerves raw—and then I began to feel—I don't know—disorientated. I could see him—not hear him—just this noise of music in my head. My heart was racing too fast and I . . ." He stopped. The trust was impossible to articulate. He went over to the desk. "Look —for God's sake—do you still keep whisky in that top drawer of yours?"

Ben did, but decided not to get it. Peterson, he remembered, was the managing director of Peterson's Pianos. There had been aggro before, recounted by Lowell with some bitterness. This time apparently the confrontation had been more tense than usual. "And then . . . ?" he prompted.

Lowell told him that he had resigned and didn't elaborate.

Ben wasn't surprised. Lowell had been in the job for nearly a year which, in the circumstances, showed a certain degree of staying power. Privately he and Louise had given him six months at most. They hadn't told Zoe, of course. According to Zoe a man needed work for his self-esteem: that it was rather like asking a modern-day Rembrandt to sell pots of poster paint in a shopping arcade hadn't occurred to her. And never would. He remembered that he and Louise were due to join Lowell and Zoe for a barbecue later that evening and wondered if they should opt out so that husband and wife could have their row in private.

"I think my blood pressure is up," Lowell said. "And, Jesus, do I need a drink!"

Ben, smiling, got out the sphygmomanometer. "Take off your jacket—roll up your sleeve."

Lowell's blood pressure was high, which was to be expected. Anger did that to you. Emotional problems had physical symptoms. Some of the patients waiting to see him might do better visiting a shrink. In Lowell's case the physical symptoms, the arthritis, had come first. Ben looked at his hands. The painful inflammatory stage was over, leaving a degree of distortion. The delicate touch of a concert pianist was no longer possible, but he was by no means crippled. If he could let his anger rip by thumping out some Scott Joplin on an old pub joanna it might do him a power of good.

He asked him why he didn't join the local sports club.

"What?" Lowell was getting back into his jacket. He'd heard, but didn't believe it. Was Ben being facetious?

"Exercise, in moderation, is therapeutic—physically—emotionally. And—no—I'm not topping you up with booze. In your present mood your driving will be hazardous and you can't risk being breathalysed."

There was a tentative tap on the door and Ben went over to open it. One of the patients had a bus to catch; did the doctor think he would be very long? Ben promised that he'd only be a couple of minutes, and turned back to Lowell. "I'll be seeing you later this evening at the barbecue—unless you'd rather we didn't come?"

Lowell had forgotten the barbecue. On the whole, it was better to have Ben and Louise there. Zoe would have bought the steaks and her mood would be worse if they weren't used. This whole situation is trivialised, he thought. I came here for help and then couldn't ask for it. To communicate one's deepest feelings, even when they

were normal and understandable, demanded a rare sensi-
tivity in the listener. Much more so when the situation
was frightening and bizarre. He wished he could reach
out to Zoe, but the barriers had been up between them
for a long time. Facing her this evening would be difficult;
he knew not to expect any warmth or sympathy there.

He told Ben he'd see him later as arranged.

The doctor put a comforting hand on his shoulder as he
walked with him to the door. "The symptoms will go,"
he said, "when you're calm. Frustration is a hell of a
thing. There aren't any pills or potions for it. You were
wise to throw up your job. Zoe should see the wisdom of
your decision—given time." Ben sounded as if he believed it but Lowell wasn't reassured. Ben didn't know
Zoe as he knew her. Nothing was smooth and easy any
more.

Zoe arrived home half an hour before her husband and
made a quick inspection of the downstairs rooms. Today
was Mrs. Hayman's cleaning day and she had asked her
to collect all the brass and polish it. She had, satisfactorily, so that small bright patches gleamed here and there.
The house, pseudo-Georgian, was without character, but
pleasant. It was one of five on the Long Ashton Road just
outside Bristol, convenient for the city and not too far
from open country. The gardens at the front were open-
plan and she had persuaded Lowell to put some fencing
up—or rather to get Ben to put some fencing up while he
watched. Ben cheerfully acknowledged that his kids
could be a nuisance—and the fence would keep them in
—so both families had gone halves on the cost. They had
been neighbours for nearly ten years and the friendship
had survived proximity. During Louise's last two preg-
nancies Zoe had helped as much as her busy practice had
allowed—mainly preparing snacks in Louise's untidy
kitchen, and keeping an eye on the eldest child. In return

Louise was a sympathetic listener when she needed to off-load her worries about Lowell. During his period of unemployment he had amused himself by composing and playing the compositions, to the best of his ability, on the Bechstein grand in the sitting room. She had persuaded him to take some music pupils from the local school in the evenings, but that hadn't worked. He insisted on perfection and scared the wits out of the kids when he didn't get it. Not that he ever said anything. Just got up and glowered over by the window until they slunk out. She had repaid the parents out of her own pocket. All this she had told Louise who, oddly, had been amused. In some ways she and Lowell were alike—impractical—depending on their partners for survival.

When Mrs. Hayman cleaned downstairs she didn't touch the bedrooms, but of course she looked at them. Zoe had tidied around quickly before leaving the house in the morning and had warned Lowell not to leave the bathroom in a mess. He got up at the last minute, reluctant to drive to a job he didn't like. She knew this but didn't encourage him to complain. She didn't love dentistry either—who would?

The bathroom, tiled in pale green with darker floral sprays, looked reasonable. She stripped off and showered, carefully pulling the matching green bath cap over her hair. Her hairdresser had given her too strong a perm and Ben had told her the tight curls looked like popcorn. Had Lowell told her she would have minded. From Ben it sounded warmly funny. She and Ben were easy together; he had a normal healthy attitude to life. Had he been in Lowell's situation he would have acted positively of his own volition. Lowell had to be chivvied into accepting what had to be accepted.

She got out of the shower and dressed for the barbecue, not caring much what she wore. Thank God today was

Friday. She was tired. But Lowell wouldn't notice. He never did.

He did notice, though. And surprised her by telling her to sit down while he poured the drinks. This was meant to be a preliminary to breaking the news, but it didn't work out like that. As she sat and sipped her gin and tonic she saw the sweat marks on his suit. The May evening was warm, but not that warm. So there was another emotional crisis. She didn't want to hear about it. Not yet. If possible, not ever.

She threw up word barriers by talking about the cottage they had planned to see this weekend. A drive into the Cotswolds would be pleasant—for both of them—she said. She'd had a busy week at the clinic. Demanding, fractious patients. No let-up. But few jobs were perfect. She wasn't complaining. Not really. What was the point? You just had to get on with it, hadn't you? At least they had the weekend to relax.

Relax, he thought. Christ! It might be easier to tell her later. Impossible now. He offered to get the barbecue lit before changing his clothes. "Your suit will need cleaning," she said, and got up quickly before the delicate topic could be pursued. "You'll find a clean shirt in the airing cupboard."

He watched her as she left the room. Once, a long time ago, she had sat in the front row while he gave his concerts and her eyes had shone. Had they needed success to keep on loving each other?

They had both got their degrees at Edinburgh University, but he had graduated two years ahead of her and was already beginning to make a name for himself when she qualified. He had been performing in Edinburgh when she got her B.D.S. and she'd invited him as a casual friend to her celebration party. After that the relationship had developed, although she didn't like music as much as she pretended to. Well—fair enough. He couldn't rustle up enthusiasm for her job either. Despite that, the sexual side was all right. Surely rather better than all right? But it wasn't now.

He told her that night after the barbecue was over—a rather strained atmosphere—Ben and Louise anxious to be gone. They were lying in bed, side by side, not touching, He didn't tell her about his reaction to Peterson.

"I'm sorry," she said in the darkness, "that your job bored you."

He was silent.

"I know," she went on, "that a sales executive isn't on the same level as an artiste."

"Salesman," he said, "and *artiste* sounds like a Punch and Judy man."

"After all that Sir Howard did for you . . ."

"He got his knighthood for selling peas."

"Do you have to mock everything?"

"Just being factual."

He wished she would cry—or even shout at him—so that he could take her in his arms and try to comfort her. Instead he sensed that she was ice-cold in her misery.

"Had you been sacked," she said, "I could have borne it."

"Resignation sounds a great deal better," he pointed out. "You can tell your friends that your husband, a sales executive, resigned because promotion to the Board of Directors didn't seem imminent."

She knew it was intended sarcastically but derived a grain of comfort from it. That was precisely what she would tell her friends, particularly her business partner, an elderly woman dentist who remembered Lowell in his heyday and tended to be embarrassingly sympathetic about what she called his tragic downfall.

She began thinking practically. "We won't be able to afford Mrs. Hayman twice a week."

"I'll clean the bloody brass."

"Or Manders for the garden."

"I'll mow the bloody lawn."

"It's as well there's no mortgage."

"Yes, we have a roof."

It was unfortunate, they both thought, that in their present mood they had to share it.

TWO

Saturday dawned tenderly—weatherwise. Lowell had slept very little and he got up at six, made himself coffee, and went out into the garden. Ribbons of mist touched the grass in places, softening the green to a delicate grey. Beds of geraniums blazed like small neat fires along the edge of the lawn. Everything here was contained, tidy. Unlike next door where Louise had pegged her eldest boy's running shorts on the line and next to them half a dozen of the baby's nappies. They were all quite wet with morning dew. Louise was a comfortable woman and a comforting one—earth mother personified. Had Ben transgressed and been kicked out of medicine she wouldn't have lain all night in their matrimonial bed totally absorbed by her own pain.

Did children help a marriage? In his and Zoe's case probably not. She was career-orientated. And as she had been saying for the last few years, wasn't it a good thing she had one? She would be saying it now, louder than ever.

Don't let your anger rise.

Practise being a suburban house-husband. Keep this neat little piece of suburban garden neat. Earn your keep by deadheading a few of those roses over there.

He didn't.

When Zoe got up at seven-thirty she could hear him playing desultory tunes on the piano. She felt a pang of pity, but it turned quickly to irritation. His musical expertise had ended, she wanted to tell him; he should stop hankering after what had gone.

She called through from the kitchen. "Do you want bacon for breakfast?"

"Can we afford it?"

Damn it, she thought. But she knew it was her own fault. Breakfast that morning was even more muted than usual.

There was no reason to defer driving to the cottage as planned. The trip would give the day some purpose. It would also help them to speak to each other fairly naturally again. They decided to use her Datsun rather than his Volvo and were careful not to say that it used less petrol. Normally she drove her car when they shared it; today with unusual tact she got into the passenger seat. It was a small gesture, but one he understood.

"Eventually," he said, "everything will be all right." He reached out and gently touched her cheek with the back of his hand.

"Yes," she answered unconvincingly.

He didn't believe it either, but gestures had to be made.

Thoughts of the cottage cheered him a little. Inheriting it quite unexpectedly, on the death of Mary Marshall, an elderly relative he hadn't known, had been like a minor win on the Pools. Very minor, according to the solicitor. Ever since the letter had arrived he had painted mind-pictures of it—all different—all attractive—a longed-for rural retreat where music could be composed in total privacy.

It took them two hours driving and searching before they eventually found their inheritance—a decaying cottage set amidst biscuit-coloured hills a few miles from

Fairford. It was called Green Pastures. "Yea, though I walk through the valley of the shadow of death, thou leadest me to this!" Zoe intoned, surveying it crossly. It had been impossible to drive any further than the bottom field and the cottage, approached by a path through rank high grass, was nearly a quarter of a mile further on. According to the villagers who had directed them, the cottage was known locally as Marshall's place. It had been empty for three years.

Marshall's Place. Lowell gave it a capital *P* in his mind. His place. His coveted—dreamed-about—bloody joke of a place. The gate was off its hinges and leaned into a bush of purple fuchsia. Dog daisies and nettles lapped the rotting window sills. Up here by the front door it was like standing in a hot saucer of sunlight, the hills gently rising towards windbreaks of elms.

"Despite the area, it's only worth about five thousand," Zoe conjectured, "to someone mad enough to buy it."

Inside, it was only slightly better. There was no mould on the walls. It smelt damp, but wasn't running with moisture. There were the remains of burnt logs in the stone fireplace—someone had obviously lit a fire here from time to time. A heavy oak beam spanned the ceiling, which flaked in places but didn't sag. Dusty rush matting obscured part of the flagged floor; Lowell pulled it aside, and was relieved to find that it wasn't hiding cracks or holes. Facing the fireplace was a shabby sofa covered with faded chintz, and two chairs, not matching, stood to the side of it.

Zoe was the first to notice the ancient piano standing in an alcove between the living-room and the bedroom. Her humour surfaced. "By God, you can't escape them, can you?" She opened the lid and tried to play "Three Blind Mice" with her right index finger. Most of the notes stuck. "Only good for firewood," Lowell said, "like some of the rubbish Peterson wanted me to sell." It was a wonder the tramp, or whoever had been living in the place, hadn't already chopped it up.

Aware that the reminder was unwise, he left Zoe and went through to inspect the bedroom. It was austerely furnished with a teak wardrobe, one chair and an iron bedstead with no mattress. The curtains on the small window were the same chintz as the covering on the sofa, but more faded. They had once been blue. The window was slightly opened at the top and a strong scent of a herb he didn't recognise blew in.

His initial disappointment was slowly giving way to an unexpected feeling of tranquillity. It was peaceful here. Like the end of the line.

Zoe was inspecting the lean-to by the back door when he rejoined her. "I suppose this is where your relative cooked." She indicated a paraffin stove standing by a filthy sink. There was no tap. Water came from an indoor pump, and a channel in the floor carried spills into a covered drain-pipe exiting through the wall.

Not salubrious.

The privy at the bottom of the garden, next to a shed of cobwebbed and rusty tools, was positively objectionable.

Lowell wandered around the garden and surveyed the countryside beyond. The sky, turquoise and flecked with small clouds, blended in the distance with a field of quietly moving Charolais cattle the colour of cream. For the first time since his frightening reaction to Peterson he felt at ease with himself. The cottage, despite its drawbacks, in some indefinable way welcomed him. It was a possession worth working on, restoring. Here, he sensed, he would heal.

Zoe, picking her way carefully through the brambled grass, reached the perimeter wall and stood behind him. "It's a total write-off, isn't it?" The question was rhetorical.

"I wouldn't say that."

"You mean the land might be of some value?" She sounded surprised. "But there's not much of it, and there isn't proper access."

"Worse places have been done up."

"Yes, but think of the cost. It would have to be gutted and rebuilt."

"I don't think so. The roof looks sound. Cotswold tiles. And the walls seem solid. No subsidence."

"There's no electricity or drainage."

"People have lived here without."

"You mean your peculiar relative?"

"And others before her. According to the solicitor, she came here in the thirties."

"And didn't do a thing to it."

"She probably didn't have the cash."

"And neither do we."

Here we go again, he thought, but this time without irritation. "If it were done up and made reasonably presentable it could be marketable," he suggested. "If it's too remote to be connected up for electricity, whoever buys it could install his own generator."

"It's too small for that sort of expense."

"Yes—as it stands. But it could be enlarged."

"What about water? No one's going to buy a place with a pump and a revolting outside lavatory."

"Someone seeing the potential might. It could be made to look attractive without spending much. Artists—writers—go for this sort of place. They would pay a premium for the solitude." And musicians, he thought.

Zoe sensed his enthusiasm and was astonished. Apart from the decaying condition of the cottage, its atmosphere was inimical. She felt much happier out here in the open air than inside it.

"It gives me the creeps." She looked nervously towards the bedroom window. "I feel I'm being watched."

It was his turn to be surprised. She wasn't usually

imaginative. If there were a watcher, it had to be a friendly one. Suddenly he felt warm with well-being.

They had lunch in Fairford on the way back and discussed it over Dover sole. (Can we afford the most expensive item on the menu? Don't ask.) He said that he wouldn't mind having a go at putting the cottage right. Replace the window frames, for instance. Get the gate back on its hinges. A lick of paint here and there.

She didn't take him seriously. He had never done manual labour before. His hands were too precious.

Not any more, he told her bitterly.

The arthritis, then?

Not bad enough to stop him. Besides, the exercise could be good. Ben had said so only the other day.

He didn't know the first thing about it.

He could learn, couldn't he? And if he made a cock-up in trying, he couldn't make the place any worse.

That was true.

They left it at that, without coming to a decision, and went to look at the stained glass in Fairford church. His suggestion. Not a good one. Zoe stood and gazed up at the West Window showing the picture of the Eternal Pit. The damned, all women, were being prodded into it by lively looking demons.

Lowell spent Sunday morning in bed with *The Sunday Times* and *Observer.* And thought. The cottage wasn't discussed at all. He had two alternatives. One was to stay here—and rot with boredom. The other was to go to the cottage and see what happened. He had no faith in his ability as a handyman, but that didn't matter. The place had calmed him yesterday, and if anything did happen, it would be a quiet sliding forward into something rather pleasant. Wouldn't it? And what did he mean by that? An unfussed separation from Zoe. If he went anywhere else it would be a statement of intent—a cause of aggro. At present he couldn't take any more aggro—not after Peterson. In time he might.

He got up and bathed. And stayed in the soapy water a long time. He was normally fastidious in his person. It would be necessary to buy some sort of bath for the cottage. In the two centuries or so of the cottage's life people had bathed in it. Slipper baths—was that what they were called? The sort miners used to put in front of the fire. Any sort of large container would do. Peace of mind was more important than creature comforts. He'd need a small fridge, one using bottled gas. Were there such things? Probably. He'd take his books with him. He hadn't read poetry for a long time. Poetry was soothing. And he'd take his radio.

He shaved, dressed casually in dark blue denims and T-shirt, and went down to see how the roast was getting on. Zoe had told him to turn the heat down at twelve-thirty. The kitchen had every modern convenience, but Zoe had been planning to get a new cooker. Now she wouldn't. Another cause of aggro. Prodded by guilt, he went into the dining-room and laid the table.

When she came home from church she told him he had used the wrong table-cloth—the damask was for when they entertained, the linen for everyday. Between them they unlaid it.

That evening they dined with a couple who had recently come to live in the area. Both were accountants. Money, a sore topic, wasn't discussed. They tried to draw Lowell out about his music, an even sorer topic, but they weren't to know. He responded politely but felt depressed.

Until he thought of his cottage again.

On Monday morning, after Zoe had left for her dental practice, Lowell drove out and had another look at it. The feeling of peace, on his own here without Zoe, was even stronger. It was like a warm dry hand reaching out from somewhere and holding his. Today a light breeze disturbed the leaves, which tumbled over each other, catching the light. A bitter smell of nasturtiums spiced the sweetness of a trailing dog rose. Nothing cloyed. He went inside to inspect the living-room and bedroom and make a list of necessities. The place had to be scrubbed through; perhaps someone in the village would do it.

The drive to Mardale took him along the Cotswold ridge, where the views were wide and level. The village, little more than a hamlet, was down a secondary road. Its single street of terraced Cotswold houses and a few small shops was narrow and parking was only possible in a lay-by near the post office. He put the Volvo there and went in.

The postmistress smiled kindly at him, but wasn't helpful. People around here, she said, "did" for themselves. "In any case," she added, "Marshall's place is too much off the beaten track, and from what I've heard it's in a bad state—no hot water. Besides, how can you hoover without electricity?"

He explained that what he needed was rather more basic than hoovering.

"I'm sorry, dear, I can't help you. The days of the char are over."

He resented the "dear" and then wondered why he should. She wasn't patronising him. This was the latter part of the twentieth century; the village might have an antique flavour to it—the cottage certainly did—but attitudes had changed. The Orwellian concept of equality was flawed; here it was sound and true. You did your own scrubbing. It was as simple as that.

He asked if letters were delivered to the cottage.

She turned and put a dozen packets of cigarettes onto the shelf behind her before answering. "In the three years I've been here, the cottage has been empty. A local

postwoman does the rounds. It's part of her job contract
to deliver within the area—but if it came to delivering at
Marshall's place, I just don't know."

He asked her what she meant, but she refused to elaborate.

The post office also sold newspapers and general gro-
ceries. Everything, she told him, had to be fetched. He
sensed that she was curious about him and appreciated
that she hadn't voiced her curiosity. She was a plump
woman of about forty with carefully styled blond hair
and too-perfect dentures. In no way was she part of the
rural dream.

"I'm a Marshall," he told the postmistress, "so I suppose you'll keep on calling the cottage that. I inherited it
from the former owner plus a few pieces of furniture."
He told her about the wood ash in the grate. "Did Miss
Marshall have an arrangement with anyone in the village
to keep the place aired?"

"Not to my knowledge. I haven't discussed her with
anyone."

He wondered if she were being evasive—all villagers
were supposed to gossip.

"Are there any tramps around here—anyone who
might want to use an empty cottage occasionally for shel-
ter?"

"I couldn't tell you."

Couldn't? Or wouldn't? Either way, it didn't matter.
He thanked the woman and left the shop, still feeling that
nothing could take the shine off his new possession.

Three days later he sold the Volvo and bought a van. Zoe,
driving home at five-thirty on Thursday evening, saw it
parked in the driveway. And didn't know who owned it.
Ben's six-year-old son, Christopher, was bouncing a red
ball against its rusting yellow door, and Louise had just

come out to stop him. "Lowell will slay you," she scowled at him and winked at Zoe.

"Lowell? It's not Lowell's." Zoe read Louise's expression. Oh, Christ, it was!

Louise nodded solemnly, then smiled. This latest crisis in the Marshall household had its funny side. It was nothing for Zoe to be so fraught about. For the first time for months Lowell looked happy.

"Apparently he needed something larger than the Volvo to carry stuff," she said. "Or so he told me when he arrived an hour or so ago."

Zoe looked at the empty garage. "Where's the Volvo?"

Louise, removing herself and her young son from the field of battle, mumbled that Christopher's tea was ready and that she'd left the baby unattended on the sofa. "I'll see you later." With soft words and a gin and tonic and a strong desire to slap you. Your man has a new toy. Enthuse.

Lowell had all his arguments ready and after Zoe's initial explosion voiced them quietly. They were standing in the kitchen, facing each other across the table. He had just finished making a mug of coffee for himself when she arrived. The Volvo had fetched two and a half thousand, he told her, which for its age was a fair price. The van, five years old, had cost six hundred. Also a fair price. On the deal the profit amounted to one thousand, nine hundred. Paints, tools and other necessities shouldn't cost more than a hundred or so. They were better off by one thousand eight hundred. Not bad work for a few days' unemployment.

He pushed his coffee towards her. Would she like it? He hadn't drunk any yet.

No, she wouldn't. She pushed it back. Her eyes, very blue, always darkened in anger. Now they were almost black.

He went on talking. So—from the financial point of

view—the deal was a good one. It had also been a wise move to sell the Volvo before it was stolen. As the cottage had no proper access, whatever vehicle he used would have to be parked by the bottom field. The van was less tempting to thieves than a quality car, but if it was stolen it wouldn't matter so much. While he had it he would put it to practical use carrying whatever he needed to the cottage—such as a bath and a mattress.

Such as *what?*

He told her he'd seen a bath in a junkyard. An invalid's. Very short and with a seat in it. It would fit in the lean-to. He was picking it up tomorrow. The mattress was the one they'd stored in the box room when they'd bought the new one. He'd probably take the base from the spare room as well.

She was beginning to shake.

"Are you trying to tell me you're leaving?"

Oh, no, not at all, he soothed. But it was very much cheaper in the long run to stay in the cottage while he did the repairs there. The daily journey, apart from being tiring, would consume a lot of petrol. He'd spend weekends at home, of course.

She didn't know how to take it—or what to say.

He went on smoothly. "As for the van, if the look of it offends you, it will just about fit the garage if you leave the Datsun out. So it will only be rather embarrassing coming and going on Saturdays and Mondays." He resisted making a quip about the artiste to artisan image. He'd needled her enough.

Zoe shook her head, for once speechless. He could dress up the situation in any words he wanted to, but this was a deliberate separation. She glanced up at the defaced wall tiles behind him where he had been trying to put up a shelf. It was easier to express her feelings about that.

Her voice shook with contained fury. "For God's sake, if you want to do any more practising, don't do it here."

. . . .

In a fortnight the cottage was habitable. Lowell had
scrubbed the floors and blistered his hands, so the painting had to wait. Ben had reminded him to have the water
analysed. It was pure. The sink had been thrown out and
replaced by a junkyard one, which was better. The privy
now housed a chemical closet and half a dozen rolls of
toilet paper kept in a plastic box safe from spiders. The
expensive items were the cooker and fridge, both run on
bottled gas. They could later be sold, he told Zoe, and she
wondered if he meant it.

It was her idea that they should have a house-warming
party on Lowell's first night there—a Monday—and ask
Ben and Louise. She wanted them to see the dump Lowell
had committed himself to. "It's not much better than a
hovel," she confided to Louise, "but it's not just that
which bothers me—it's the atmosphere." She hadn't been
able to explain her fears. "You'll see what I mean when
you go there."

The party began at seven. Mellow evening light
flooded the living-room like yellow water on a lonely
shore. It was too hot for a fire, so they put the beer cans
on the stone hearth. The food—ham, sausages, garlic
bread and an assortment of fruit—was laid out on a
plastic cloth covering the rickety table Lowell had found
in the shed.

It was by no means a jolly occasion. Lowell, sensing
Zoe's motives, had agreed to the party only reluctantly.
The cottage wasn't ready for visitors. Nor was he. He
wanted to be left in peace here. Guests, even when they
were old friends, were an intrusion.

Ben, normally gregarious, found himself striving for
words—social chit-chat—and knew he was being trite.
Louise talked about the children—a too-easy topic for her
and one she usually avoided. Edward, at ten, was due to
start soon at his prep school. Horrendous, wasn't it?

What were they doing to the poor child? Were they crazy? It was supposed to sound light-hearted, but it didn't come out that way. She caught Zoe looking at her and looked away. Yes, she thought, you were right. There is something wrong here.

Before leaving she took a walk down the garden to the privy. The countryside was gently grey, the trees charcoal against the bronze sky. In another hour the light would be gone. She was afraid to go into the privy and stopped by the door. She was being ridiculous. It was disgustingly crude, but that wasn't the reason. She didn't want to be enclosed anywhere here on her own. From this side of the cottage she couldn't see the living-room window and felt a panic need for human contact. But more physically she also needed to empty her bladder, and did so, crouching in the high grass, her heart beating. When she returned to the cottage she looked at Zoe again and in a rare moment of voiceless communication the two women understood each other and were in sympathy.

Why, in God's name, Louise wondered, does Lowell like it so much? He's wearing the place like an old familiar coat—and he wants us gone. "Have a care, love." She reached up and kissed him as he took them to the door.

He was surprised by her demonstrativeness and knew he couldn't take his leave of Zoe without showing her equal warmth. He took her in his arms and briefly kissed her on the lips. "Are you sure you won't stay the night?"

"I'm sorry. I can't." *It's not that I won't. I can't.*

He sensed what she hadn't said and released her gently.

Ben's leave-taking was coolly practical. "In a couple of months," he said, "you'll have it looking good enough to put on the market." It was supposed to be consoling, a friendly leave-taking, but Lowell couldn't get rid of them fast enough.

That night he had the best sleep he had had for months.

His body felt sated and relaxed, as if he had made love. These days sex with Zoe was infrequent, always perfunctory, and never left him feeling like this. He woke once— and reached out for someone who wasn't there. The room was very dark and smelt of herbs. He slept again, deeply, dreamlessly.

When he awoke it was ten o'clock. The day was as bright as buttercups and he skipped breakfast to go walking. The hills rolled in all directions, but were higher to the west. He wondered what lay beyond them. One day he'd climb over there and see. Hungry by now, he returned to the cottage and boiled a couple of eggs and made toast. He ate them, sitting on a canvas folding chair from home (but this was home) in the wild garden. Bees sucked nectar from a bush of herbs behind him near the cottage wall—they lay on it thick as peas in a pod and grumbled at him when he moved but were too intent on their feast to leave it. He supposed he ought to get up and do something—like scything the grass. But why bother— the day was too hot. A cold shower would be pleasant, but not possible. He filled a bucket with water from the pump, took it outside, stripped, and splashed it over him, drenching his thick dark hair, running it over his torso, his legs, splashing it over his feet. Then he dried off in the sun and dozed, still naked, like primitive Adam in an unpeopled wilderness.

Wednesday was cooler. He tried to fix the gate, but he needed cement to hold the new strut and he hadn't any. The fuchsia bush had been embracing it for a long time without detriment, so leave it be. His hands were better, the blisters healing, so tomorrow he would disturb the trim line of paint tins by removing one and using it on the living-room wall. In the meantime he played a cassette of *Acis and Galatea,* Handel's pastoral serenade, and several cassettes of excerpts from his own piano performances. Here at last, in the cottage, he could play them without pain.

By the end of the week he'd emulsioned one wall of the living room white—and wished he hadn't. It had changed the character a little, like putting one of Zoe's surgical coats on top of a tattered but subtly coloured dress. A soft shade of beige would be better. Next week he'd change the white for something more appropriate. Was it worth it? Yes. The cottage was in partnership with him. It had its own strong personality. White wouldn't do.

When he went home he tried to tell Zoe something of this, but she looked at him mystified. He changed the subject. "Have you planned anything for the weekend?"

She reminded him that they were having a dinner party on Sunday evening—a return visit of the accountants they'd been to.

"Must we?"

"We're under an obligation."

"A social treadmill: I feed you—you feed me. Has it ever occurred to you that so-called civilised behaviour is avoidable?"

She ignored him. And went on doing so for most of the weekend. Lowell drove back to the cottage on Monday, pleased to be returning. The warm dry spell had given way to a period of heavy rain and the smell of damp in the cottage was strong. He would have to light a fire, but there was no fuel.

He examined the piano and reluctantly decided it was beyond repair. He would happily have disposed of some of Peterson's modern rubbish, but with this old instrument he felt more than a touch of sadness. It had been good in its day. Loved by someone, perhaps. The brass candle holders above the keyboard were intricately wrought. He removed them. In winter they could be put to practical use. It was necessary to be practical. He played a few chords. The keys were as stiff as his bloody hands. No hope of recovery. Face up to it. Get on with the job. You're not vandalising. You need firewood. Because of its size he decided to take the piano apart, piece by piece, where it was, and unscrewed it like a surgeon performing a delicate operation. Or a pathologist removing sections of a corpse. The analogy was unpleasant. He wished he hadn't thought of it.

Woodworm had chewed away most of the back panel and a section was covered with a piece of dark green serge cloth, which in turn was shredded. He ripped it off. A small gilt photo frame that must have stood on the piano at one time and then fallen through the torn material descended the last few inches onto the stone floor.

Lowell picked it up. Thick grime on the cracked glass obscured the photograph. He turned it over and carefully prised away the rusted nails holding the frame.

Instinctively knowing that this find was important, he sat back on his heels savouring the moment. Rain had made the cottage dark. This should be looked at in the light. He took it to the window and then, very gently, removed the sepia print.

As he held the photograph in his hands he was powerfully aware that this was the beginning of something—he didn't know what.

THREE

It was of a girl dressed in the fashion of the late nineteenth century. Her hair was dark, the thick curls pulled back from her oval face. Her lips formed a gentle smile and her eyes were looking intently into his as if she were probing his mind and liking what she found there.

There had been events in his life that had stayed in his memory—clearly and strongly—never to be forgotten. The good and the bad vividly imprinted. The fabric of change. He felt a shock of intense pleasure. By God, she was lovely.

He laughed back at the smiling face. "Hello," he said. "Hello, whoever you are." And, as he spoke, Lowell felt impelled to find out more.

Edwin Leeson rented rooms for his photography business in a small side street off the Haymarket in Bristol's busy shopping centre. His reputation as a good professional had been growing over the years and in time he hoped to be able to afford more impressive premises. His ambition was to concentrate on portraiture and not bother with the run-of-the-mill developing and printing side of the business. Customers' holiday snaps bored him. The present craze for reproducing old sepia photographs, however, was another matter. Family trees adorned with the fruits of photographers long dead were a tantalising insight into the past.

And this photograph was superb.

"It's a helluva good one," he told Lowell.

"That's why I brought it to you."

The Marshalls and the Leesons had been friends—or rather, friendly acquaintances—for a few years. Leeson had taken commercial and press photographs of Lowell when he performed in Bristol and Bath. He hadn't been a good sitter, intensely disliking what he regarded as the razzmatazz side of serious music, but Leeson had soothed him into accepting what had to be with the balm of small talk. After several sessions they found they got on well enough to end the sittings with a drink in a neighbouring pub. Leeson's wife Jane helped with the clerical work and acted as receptionist. She and Zoe had discovered a mutual interest in flower arranging one day while Lowell was submitting to the purgatory of posing in the room at the back. After that they met each winter at a crafts club and occasionally at each other's houses.

This, Leeson thought, was no Zoe. And no relative of Zoe's. This girl was a cracker.

He asked Lowell who she was.

"I don't know." Then he explained about the cottage and where he'd found the photograph.

Leeson was intrigued. "The last one a customer brought in was found down the back of a sofa. It had been there fifty years or more. He bought the sofa in the antique market in Clifton and was stripping it to have it re-covered. That was of a man—goatee beard—posed by a chiffonier." He looked more closely at the photograph. "This girl is posing by something, too, though it's obscured by the mount. Any objection if I remove it?"

Lowell felt a stab of apprehension. "For God's sake be careful. Don't tear it." He turned his back and pretended to be interested in a family group posed against a wall of books.

"You may look now," Leeson said, amused. "The lady is unscathed."

Without the mount the photograph showed that the girl was resting part of her right hand on a stone urn—the rest of the urn was off the picture. "An unnecessary prop," Leeson criticised, "badly placed. The photographer probably thought the same when he developed it and arranged the mount to cover it. Beautiful hands, hasn't she?" Belatedly aware that the comment was hurtful, he felt embarrassed by his lack of tact. Hands were a taboo subject. He should have remembered.

Lowell agreed. They were beautiful: small and well-shaped. Healthy. Normal. Not like mine at all, he thought bitterly.

Since his discovery he had dreamed of her twice. They had lain side by side not touching. In the dreams she had been virginal. Pure.

"A whore?" Leeson mused.

Not noticing Lowell's shocked expression he went on examining the photograph. "Well—who knows? Judging by the eyes I'd say she'd been around. And she had something going with the photographer, you can tell by the way she looked at him."

Lowell wished he would stop. *She looks at me. At me!*

It took him a moment or two to control his anger at Leeson's comments and speak calmly. "In those days didn't the photographers drape themselves behind their cameras with a black cloth?"

Leeson grinned. "With an ugly mug like mine it could be an advantage. Perhaps she was thinking of her lover."

Lowell abruptly asked him if he could date the photograph.

"Approximately the time Conan Doyle was clicking away as a gifted amateur. Somewhere between eighteen seventy and eighteen eighty. And speaking of Doyle—if you'd like me to do a bit of sleuthing I've a friend who's an archivist. He might pinpoint the date more accurately."

Lowell said that the approximation would do.

Any sleuthing would take place at the cottage and its environs—by him. Leeson's attitude had made him feel extraordinarily jealous and protective of her. She was his concern—no one else's.

"I don't want it lent to anyone. I brought it to you so that you could enlarge it for me. I want you to make it as big as you can without losing any of the definition."

Leeson was surprised. Zoe's sitting-room, as he remembered it, had one picture only—a Lowry print. "Does Zoe like it so much?"

Lowell explained that she hadn't seen it. "It's a gift," he lied, "so I don't want it sent home. I'll fetch it when it's ready. How long will it take?"

Leeson, sensing urgency, said he'd do it in a week. He was extremely busy, but this was something special. The girl in the photograph was a demanding presence. It was difficult to believe she was no longer alive.

It was midweek when Lowell left the photograph with Leeson. Wednesday—the middle day of five days of blissful solitude. Zoe was forgettable when he was away from her, but when they were together her brooding resentment was hard to ignore, and petty irritations were magnified out of all proportion. Since acquiring the cottage he had done very little to it. On Mondays he rested his bruised spirits after being rubbed raw at the weekends. On Tuesdays, Wednesdays and Thursdays he sat around —or went walking, but never far. On Fridays the prospect of the weekend jangled his nerves and prodded him into activity so that he could report to Zoe about the work in progress. So far he had successfully dissuaded her from coming to look. All it amounted to was a half-hearted attempt to replace a piece of rotting skirting board—and a repainting of the white wall so that it was near its original shade of diluted beer. But not near enough. Hands off, the cottage seemed to say. Stop tinkering. I'm all right as I am. Leave me be.

But it wasn't tinkering to fix a piece of corkboard to the bedroom wall so that the photograph of the Girl could be attached to it when it was ready. For this he needed an awl and some plugs and could pick up his car insurance documents at the same time. It had just gone three o'clock and Zoe would be off the premises until five.

Mrs. Hayman had just washed the terrazzo tiles in the kitchen and was now sitting in the dining-room reading one of Zoe's fashion journals and drinking a glass of sherry when he walked in. They looked at each other with a degree of alarm. He had forgotten it was her cleaning day and apologised for startling her. "I came for an awl." It sounded incomprehensible. Spelling helped. She jumped up guiltily, her heavy features flushing. She wanted to say, "Don't tell Mrs. Marshall," but couldn't bring herself to do so. He wanted to tell her the same, but discretion prevailed. Together they found the tool box, which had been moved from the boiler room to the utility room. There were three various-sized awls in it, but no Rawlplugs. He should have gone to the ironmongers in the first place and left the insurance documents until the weekend. "I need to make a hole," he said, "in the sort of wall that crumbles when you breathe on it. Which would you advise?" Mrs. Hayman, aware that he was making conversation just to be kind, felt the last of her guilt dissolve. He was a nice man who had once made nice music. He was now, according to his snooty wife, improving a summer residence he had recently inherited. "Your handyman," she said, "will probably need them all." "Then he shall have them," said Lowell.

It was after six when he returned to the cottage. Blending with the familiar smell of dust and old timbers was another stronger scent. He put the corkboard and tools on the floor and sniffed like a setter on the trail of an obscure beast. Not an unpleasant smell. Pervasive. It was years since he had last smelt it. On one of his foreign tours? No —in Edinburgh—in his student days. *Cannabis.*

An audacious intruder had come into his cottage to *smoke grass*—and light the fire; there was still a spark of life in a piece of charred wood in the grate.

Had he come home earlier he would have walked in on whoever it was. As he had walked in on Mrs. Hayman. That encounter had embarrassed them both. The poor old biddy could have downed a bottle of scotch for all he cared, but embarrassment was catching. This encounter would have been on a different level. Interesting—perhaps amusing. Life here played a different sort of music. The high sharp chords of suburban living, where a filched glass of sherry mattered, gave way to deeper, more mysterious notes. He was curious, not angry. The cottage, once the bolts were shot on the doors, was impregnable. By day, the bolts drawn back, anyone could get in. He could, of course, have a secure lock fitted. But why bother? In no way did he feel menaced. The fugue one day might take form.

Zoe arrived home an hour after Lowell had left. She was tired after a difficult day—an impacted wisdom tooth had broken—a couple of fractious children had resisted treatment—nothing had gone right. Mrs. Hayman's lack of effort around the house was obvious and she had been about to comment on it when the woman told her about Lowell. His unexpected arrival, she'd said, had cut into her time.

They'd had to search for the tool box.

Zoe, aware that she was being fobbed off with an excuse, was too upset to argue. Lowell had deliberately come and gone at a time when she wasn't there. He hadn't even left a note.

That evening she went next door and baby-sat while Ben and Louise went to a symphony concert at the Colston Hall. They had invited her to go, too; it would be easy enough to arrange for another sitter, they told her, but she had refused. The concerts in the old days when Lowell was star of the show had been worth attending. She was given the best seat. Was fussed over. There was no fun being an appendage of a happily married couple listening to a stranger performing. But there was, she discovered, even less fun giving a late-night bottle to Clarissa in an effort to stop her yelling.

When Ben and Louise returned they found their baby daughter asleep in a carry-cot in the sitting room and Zoe, pale and tired, dozing in a chair.

"Our neighbour," Ben told Louise at some time after midnight when the house was quiet and Zoe had gone home, "needs t.l.c."

Louise, on a high after the concert and ready for love, moved closer to him in the big double bed. Ben's tender loving care was for her. "She's frigid," she said, "that's what's wrong with her. She's buttoned up in a perpetual chastity belt. Emotionally. And Lowell can't get her out of it—if he ever wanted to. She can't feel the sort of hurt that matters, only the niggling sort. She knows all about pride—and appearance—and the discomfort of being on her own. She's introverted. It's all Zoe. No Lowell. I bet she's never thumped him out of passionate rage—or scarred him with love bites—or—" She rolled over on her back as Ben silenced her with his probing tongue and made love slowly and expertly.

"Or had an orgasm," she said drowsily, afterwards.

The finished photograph of the Girl was excellent—large, clear and with all the qualities of first-class portraiture. It didn't occur to Lowell to ask about the original photograph. He knew nothing about the enlarging process and assumed that it had been unavoidably damaged. A pity—but this beautiful image in front of him now more than compensated for its loss. Leeson for his part was careful not to mention it. Lowell had stated that he didn't want it lent to anyone, but he hadn't promised he wouldn't. This woman—this girl—whoever she was—hadn't walked through life a century ago without leaving interesting footprints. It was a hunch, he could be wrong, but Leeson had a growing feeling that a search through the newspapers of the time might reveal her identity. If it did, he could tell Lowell her name. He had seen besotted bridegrooms gazing at portraits of their brides with the same expression that Lowell had now. This was something more than artistic appraisal. It was startling and to a degree disconcerting. He seemed obsessed.

"It's wonderfully lifelike," Lowell said quietly. "You've done an extremely good job. She could be here in the room with us."

But she isn't, Leeson thought. She's what her contemporary Victorians would call a remnant of mortality—a skeleton. Dead, my friend. Dead.

He asked Lowell if he had time to come out with him for a jar.

Lowell said he hadn't—he had work to do at the cottage.

On this Wednesday he didn't go home. Zoe had been bitterly silent most of the weekend on account of his brief visit the previous week. To come and go without waiting to see her had been insulting, she had accused. It probably had been and he hadn't tried to come up with a defence; instead he had bought her a bottle of her favourite perfume and left it on the dressing-table after she had gone to work on Monday morning. It had been impossible to hand it to her. Too much like a St. Bernard rolling up with a cask of brandy several days too late. Let her find it and tell the empty house that (a) he couldn't afford it, (b) he couldn't appease her that way, and (c) what did the gesture mean, anyway? By the next weekend her mood might have improved. He doubted it, but was ceasing to care.

He had fixed the corkboard to the wall facing his bed ready to receive the enlarged photograph, and he attached it carefully with drawing pins. Leeson had suggested having it framed, but he had refused. To enclose the Girl in gilt or silver would be like drawing a chalk line around a living woman and telling her to stay inside it. A crazy idea that he kept to himself. She needed access to his bed, his dreams, his erotic imagination.

She. The Girl. Who? Anna? Esther? Harriet? Charlotte? None of the names fitted.

He wondered what colour eyes she had. Hazel? Green? Calculating like Zoe's; the finely arched eyebrows beckoned him to meet her gaze. Her dress was edged with lace at the neck and was cut demurely high, but was tight over the breasts. A leather belt encircled her waist—or perhaps the belt was made of webbing—hard to tell. A cameo brooch at the neck completed the period detail. He imagined her dressed in a deep shade of red. And then— her amused eyes watching him—he imagined her dressed in nothing at all. A gentle disrobing of a lovely creature.

A woman who had come home. This was her place. Marshall's place. His place.

When he dreamed at night now, Lowell dreamed constantly of her. Sometimes sensually, sometimes coolly as if they had been lovers a long time and had reached contentment. And when he awoke in the morning she was there, her gaze quizzical, her soft full lips half smiling.

There were times when he chided himself for behaving like an adolescent sexually aroused by a pin-up. For a man of his age and experience this was an aberration. He

knew it and didn't care. There had been other women in
his life before Zoe—and varying degrees of sexual pleasure. Zoe had been a virgin when he had married her and
he had initiated her gently and lovingly. The loving, he
guessed, had been all on his side.

And with this one—the Girl—it was all on his side. A
solo performance. A freak-out during a period of depriva-
tion.

It was the voice of reason, but he refused to believe it.
She was inside him, around him, a footfall, a smell of
warm skin, a hand in his. Her eyes registered understanding of his need. They couldn't, but they did. He talked to
her and she talked back inside his head, telling him what
he needed to be told. With her he felt whole, confident,
capable of anything.

The urge to make music had been dormant for a while,
but now—in her presence—it had reawakened. He scrib-
bled a few bars of a nocturne and whistled it softly, test-
ing its musicality, liking it. It was for her. A beginning of
something that might eventually be worthwhile. Excited
by it, pleased to be working at something he loved, he
was loath to leave the composition when the weekend
arrived.

He phoned home from a call-box in the village. There
was graffiti on the walls—a heart pierced by an arrow—a
coupling of names. The air was stale and he propped the
door open with a tattered directory.

Zoe was listening to the early evening news when the
call came through. The real world was bad enough, she
thought, as she listened to Lowell's reason for not coming
home, but his attempt to retreat into the world of music
was worse. How could he compose without a piano? He
was an instrumentalist, not a composer. He knew that, he
told her patiently, but he had a degree of ability and what
he was writing now wasn't trash. Then write it at home,
she said, not unreasonably, and try it out on the Bech-

stein. He would eventually, he promised, but not this weekend. He needed to stay here, where the atmosphere was right, and get on with it.

"If you need to get on with anything," she nagged, "then get on with improving the cottage—make it saleable—that's why you're there, isn't it? . . . Isn't it?" she repeated, half crying. He told her coldly that his small change was running out. "I'll have to ring off." She asked for the call-box number so that she could ring him back. "We've got to talk." Oh no, he thought. Oh no, Zoe. There's been too much talk. For too long. And too abrasive. He pretended not to have heard and put the phone down.

As always, contact with her unsettled him and instead of going directly back to the cottage he tried to walk off his mood. The evening was mellow and a gloss of gold touched the cornfields so that they shone like silk. He took the path to the west of the cottage and climbed towards the copse of trees, past the fields of Charolais cattle. A bull roamed amongst them, a large white creature with massive shoulders. Staying on the safe side of the wall, he kept climbing until he saw the farmhouse on the far side of the hill. It had the look of an old priory, a gracious building of Cotswold stone and much older than the byres and cow-houses surrounding it. He admired it without coveting it. A pleasant house in a pleasant landscape. Impersonal.

His own cottage, dwarfed even more by distance, was stumpy and squalid. Ugly, yet welcoming. Perhaps in Her day it had been better. The garden would have been tended—she might have sown the honeysuckle that ran rampant now along the wall. It was disconcerting to place her in the past where she belonged. He blamed Zoe. Zoe said: This is the world as it is now. *Look at it!* And for a while he looked.

· · · ·

He began retracing his steps. The van, clearly visible from up here, crouched near the bottom road like a monstrous yellow beetle. The van Zoe disliked so much. Her displeasure cast a pall over everything. It drove the music out of his head and blinded his eyes to the Girl until he could look at her again as he had looked at her before the phone call. The magic was fragile and easily broken. It was safer to break the soil.

He dug for an hour or more, clearing a patch of weeds at the bottom of the garden. The ground was soft and easy to work. A crop of something he didn't recognise had been planted here—and not so long ago. He wondered what it was and who had bothered to plant it. Later, just as he was beginning to tire, he struck harder ground and was about to give up when the spade dislodged a fragment of carved stone. He picked it up and brushed off the soil—the key pattern, entwined by vine leaves, was familiar. He felt a rush of excitement.

The evening was beginning to darken and he had to take the stone indoors and light the lamp in the bedroom before he could make the comparison. And then he was sure. It was part of the urn the Girl rested her hand upon. If he had needed any proof that she had once lived here, he had it now. All thoughts of Zoe went out of his mind. This was his reality. He fingered it, as she was fingering it in the photograph. If there was more buried in the garden he might be able to reconstruct it—it would be a labour of love—a patient putting together of something she had once touched. Feeling euphoric, he raised the lamp and smiled at her.

FOUR

Use the weekend positively, Zoe told herself. Don't just sit back and let Lowell do this to you. Make good use of his absence. Now is your chance to see Sir Howard. He got him a job before. He'll get him another. Use your gumption. Move.

It was a bright breezy Saturday morning, and the drive to Sir Howard's country house in Worcestershire was pleasant. Zoe arrived without a preliminary phone call—it was better to chance his being out than give him the opportunity of arranging to be out—and found the family at lunch. They invited her to join them, but she declined; she had had a snack on the way. She accepted coffee.

Sir Howard, sensing stress, suggested adding a dash of Cointreau to liven it—or would she prefer whisky? He called her "love" in his broad Midland accent and she felt comfortable with him.

He didn't feel altogether comfortable with her. This young woman with the frizzy hair-do and determined expression wasn't here socially. She wanted to see him about Lowell—again.

His wife had guessed this, too. It would be tactful to chat briefly over a second cup of coffee and then withdraw. Murmuring a vague excuse a short while later, she left them to it.

"How is Lowell?" Howard asked, and sat back to listen while she told him.

Sensing that he might know the truth already, Zoe didn't bother wrapping it up in a tissue of excuses. Lowell hadn't liked his job. It hadn't suited his temperament. He had resigned. Since then he had been spending his time renovating a property that had been left to him. Perhaps Howard knew about the cottage?

He had heard of it. Yes.

Mary Marshall had been related to his sister's husband's family—but other than that, he didn't know much about her. "I believe she made a living of sorts selling herbs."

Zoe described the state of the place. "In time, when Lowell has improved it, it will be sold. But not for very much. It's the long-term prospect of his unemployment that worries me. It isn't good for him emotionally. And, of course, we need the money." In case he thought she had come for a loan, she continued hastily. "My salary is adequate, though our standard of living has dropped. It's the future that bothers me. The present state of affairs just can't go on."

Can't go on for whom? Howard wondered. This very positive young woman had married his nephew when his career was on the up. In the normal way Lowell would have stayed at the top of his musical career for a long time, and they would have lived together richly—in every sense of the word. Failure was impoverishing—again in every sense of the word. The garland of success had been brutally removed and it would take a good marriage to survive its loss.

"Love him?" he asked bluntly.

The question coming from this large bluff man with the small, astute eyes was both surprising and embarrassing. Zoe looked past him and at the sweeping lawn outside the french window. "Of course."

He didn't know whether to believe her or not. Lowell was like his father had been—emotionally unstable, difficult. He had inherited his musical ability from his mother, Howard's sister. Ann's marriage into the Marshall family had ended her musical career. In those days a wife stayed at home. If there had been trauma no one knew. In today's world Lowell exposed his wounds. Could expose them.

"As you know," he said, "I pulled a few strings and got Lowell the job with the piano company." He smiled wryly, remembering Peterson's acid comment: "An act of sabotage—next time off-load him on your enemies—I'll guarantee he'll bankrupt them for you."

"I'm hoping," Zoe admitted, "that you'll pull a few strings again."

He pointed out that unemployment was rife—that Lowell was only trained for one job he could no longer do.

"I think that Lowell would be prepared to consider anything now. Preferably something in the executive line."

"Nepotism," Howard retorted drily, "is only excusable if it furthers the family business." He saw her expression, relented, and tried to be constructive. "If he took a course in business studies, familiarised himself with computers, for instance, I might find a slot for him in one of my offices. Failing that, it would have to be something pretty basic in the canning factory."

She was silent.

Mute, he guessed, with misery.

He tried harder: she was, after all, married to Ann's son. Ann, were she alive, would expect him to be more supportive. "There's a small subsidiary of my firm in Gloucester," he said. "The manager there might take him on for a trial period—and he could do a day-release course in business studies. It would lead to something

better eventually." He told her he would get the address
and telephone number from his study and to help herself
to more coffee.

In the five minutes it took him to get the information
he thought of an even better idea. The business in Hong
Kong had a limited period to run, a few dropped bricks
on the line wouldn't matter. It could carry a passenger.

"Alternatively," he told Zoe on his return, "Lowell
could go abroad." He explained the situation, but with a
degree of tact. "It's short term—but valuable experience.
Two or three years away from base might freshen his
outlook—help him to adjust."

Her hand shook as she put down the coffee cup. "That
wouldn't do at all. I don't want to lose him."

"You could go, too."

"I'm a professional woman," she pointed out stiffly. "I
couldn't leave my dental practice—just like that."

"Then tell Lowell to contact Stephenson at the
Gloucester office in a couple of weeks." He gave her the
business card. "I'll need to put in a word before Lowell
applies. And if he can dream up a likely sounding c.v.
that isn't downright dishonest, get him working on it."

He had hoped to raise a smile, but her expression was
bitter. "He has nothing to offer of any value at all."

"Except musical brilliance," Howard reminded her.
"It's still there in his head, you know. It's just that the
hands won't work to interpret it."

"Nothing of any practical value," Zoe insisted.

"Well, we can't all be dentists," Howard retorted, temporarily losing patience. For the first time he felt some
sympathy for his nephew. This girl had guts and drive
and would eventually sergeant-major her husband into
something, but for whose sake was she doing it?

"Cheer up, love," he said briskly, "life can only get
better."

"It has to," said Zoe dully. Wasn't there, Sir Howard wondered, any laughter inside her anywhere?

It was difficult for Lowell to remember which day of the week it was. Particularly as he preferred not to. With the Girl up on his wall—presiding over the cottage by day, filling his dreams by night—Saturday, the weekend as a whole, became an irrelevance, best ignored. He had, quite simply, stopped the clock and lived like his ancestors by the sun. That this healing therapy was bizarre didn't occur to him. It worked. He felt marvellous. And that was all that mattered.

He lived on packets and cans of convenience foods and dried milk. Eventually he would have to go to the village shop and stock up, but not yet. Here in his cottage and the garden there was peace. His nocturne was growing slowly like a tender plant. It was for his night-time woman. For his daytime woman he dug the garden for fragments of urn but failed to find any. It didn't matter. The air was as clear as bells. There was music in it. He smiled a lot to himself and didn't have to hide the smile with a hand over his lips; there was no one here to mock his gentle madness—if that was what it was. And he had ceased to question the possibility.

When Zoe drove over to the cottage on the Saturday afternoon, she found him raking a small pile of stones and examining them as intently as if he were on an archaeological dig. He had cleared a large area of weeds and piled them up in a heap, presumably to burn at some stage. So he *was* working—after his fashion. It was a warm day and he was stripped to his waist, his skin sun-reddened and sweaty. He looked like a navvy. Perhaps he could take his place on an assembly line after all—oil the robots. Why not? Her fury, dark and contained, conjured up the picture and derived satisfaction from it. How dare he not come home? How dare he not even telephone her?

"So you're not ill," she said caustically.

He hadn't heard her approach, and her voice, sharp and staccato, startled him. He turned quickly and looked at her. She was standing by the garden entrance where the fuchsia dripped scarlet petals over her grey high-heeled shoes. Like drops of blood, he thought.

"Ill?" he said, puzzled. "Why should I be ill?"

"You didn't come home. I worried about you." And you made a fool of me, she accused him in her mind. Louise asked about you and I didn't know what to tell her.

"So this is Saturday?" Lowell put down the spade and went over to her. "Christ! I'm sorry—I didn't realise." Duty demanded a kiss. He didn't feel dutiful. She moved away from him before he could touch her.

She preceded him into the cottage, which was still as dingy as she remembered it. What, if anything, had he done to the place? There was a dusty, sweetish smell of decay. Weak sunlight filled the room without warming it. She shivered.

He noticed. "You can't be cold. It isn't cold." And then: "Shall I light the fire for you?"

"No. We're not staying."

He ignored that. Placate her first. Make your statement of intent afterwards. He wasn't returning with her.

He watched her as she prowled around the room, cat-like in her sleek grey suit and matching blouse. Her knotted scarf in a soft shade of blue should have a bell attached to it, he thought. Ring-a-ting—I'm closing in on you, take cover.

She noticed his book of Keats on the window ledge and fingered it disdainfully. "So you're reading poetry?"

Mea culpa. It's the worst form of pornography. He bit back the sarcasm, not wanting to needle her. He had searched through Keats to find a name for the Girl, but had found nothing appropriate.

"And this, I suppose, is your musical composition?" Lowell tensed. He had left the manuscript on the table and didn't want it touched. "Just the beginning of something." He took it from her and put it in the table drawer.

"Which you can finish at home."

"No."

"What do you mean—no?"

"Which I can finish here."

"Without a piano?"

"The music is in my head."

And nothing else, she thought. His uncle had spoken of musical brilliance, but what use was that any more?

His shirt was a crumpled heap on the chair and he picked it up to put on. She had brought coldness into the room.

She noticed grass stains on the cuffs. "If you'd like to pack your shirts—anything that needs washing—we can take them with us."

"I do my own washing here—perhaps not expertly, but well enough." He sat on the chair facing the fireplace, deliberately not looking at her.

She took the chair opposite. "You've always brought your washing home."

He didn't answer.

She persisted. "Apart from last weekend when you didn't come."

He stayed silent.

"Tonight Ben and Louise have asked us round to dinner."

"Good. You'll have company."

She felt as if she were playing poker with the wrong cards. It was a hand she didn't know how to play. "Are you trying to tell me you're not coming home?"

"Just that." It was brusque, unkind, and he wished he could care, but he couldn't."

She braced herself against pain, but anger was stronger than hurt. She mustn't give way to it.

"So the cottage has become a full-time job—weekends and all." She glanced around the room. "I see you've put up some corkboard in here—what's that for? Reminders of work to be done?"

It was for the Girl when he was composing. Later, when Zoe had gone, he would take her from the bedroom wall and pin her up here. Together they made music.

He shrugged at Zoe's venom and didn't answer.

"I suppose that's why you wanted the bradawl that Wednesday you came home," she conjectured. "You should buy your own tools with the money you made on the Volvo—that was why you sold it, wasn't it, so that you could do this place up? And, by the way, there's a crack in the side window of your van. It's a wonder it hasn't been totally vandalised by now. Can't you see how ridiculous all of this is? Why not put the cottage on the market as it stands? You're never going to improve it—and you know it."

"I'm never going to sell it," Lowell said.

He had told her what she had feared he would tell her —a truth she had strenuously resisted in her mind. Of course he wasn't coming home. He was leaving her. Ditching her. For good.

It mustn't happen. She wouldn't let it happen. A troubled husband was still better than no husband. He must be made to see sense.

Her throat felt dry with nerves and it was a few moments before she could speak. She pretended to misunderstand him. "Though it will probably sell eventually—it won't be easy."

"It's mine. I'm keeping it."

"You can't possibly like it."

"Oh, but I do."

It was better not to argue. If you were in deep water

and drowning you didn't open your mouth for air until you surfaced.

He wondered at her silence, her apparent calm. Had he misjudged her? When she spoke again he knew he hadn't.

Her attack came from an unexpected direction. She had been to see his uncle, she told him, and Sir Howard thought he could help.

"Help?"

"To get you a job." Her handbag was on the floor by her feet. She stooped and opened it and handed him the address of the Gloucester firm.

It would be a beginning, she urged. He had the right connections. His uncle would see that everything went well for him—in time. All he had to do was play his part. Taking a course in business management shouldn't be difficult for him. After all, he'd been to university. True—the course had been musical and didn't relate to anything else, but that shouldn't matter. Lots of businessmen had degrees in unrelated subjects. All he needed was the will to get on with it. Bristol would have been better than Gloucester, but there was no reason why they shouldn't sell up the Bristol house and buy something midway between. In the country.

They could both commute. She didn't mind. All that mattered was that he should get on. Take on the responsibilities of a man again. Fooling around here was emasculating him. It wasn't doing him any good. He couldn't stay in this filthy place for ever. It was rotting and evil and horrible. Some cottages had a good feel to them. This one hadn't. There was something wrong here—or there had been something wrong here a long time ago. It was an old woman's house. An old crone's place. It even smelt of her. It smelt bloody!

He handed her back the Gloucester address and began

to laugh. How mistaken could she be! "Come with me." He took her by the arm, "I want to show you something."

She pulled her arm free, but followed him to the bedroom.

Had a woman lain naked on his bed she would have been less surprised. The situation would have been natural, easier to deal with.

"There's your old crone," he said. "Beautiful, isn't she?"

And she was.

Zoe stood mute in front of the photograph and Lowell looked at the two women as if they were both living. She sensed the comparison he was making and her flesh felt frozen, lifeless, as if her blood were being transfused into the other one.

He's mad, she thought. But the explanation was too simple. There was something powerful here—something she could feel but not understand. He was in love with a dead Victorian woman. *And the woman knew it.*

And if she, Zoe, could believe that, then she was mad too.

She resisted the thought and forced herself to speak naturally. "Who is she?"

"I don't know, but I believe she lived here once." He then told her about the urn.

She remembered the pile of stones he had unearthed. It hadn't been gardening zeal. His zeal, his enthusiasm, centred on Her.

She told him that she was cold—that some hot tea would help. While he made it she would gather up some of his clothes to be washed and he could collect them the following weekend.

Her apparent low-key reaction to the Girl put him off guard. If she insisted on gathering up his laundry, there was no point in making an issue of it. It was probably bait to get him home. He told her there might be a couple of soiled shirts in the wardrobe.

She fetched them and put them on the bed; then, when she could hear him pumping water for the kettle, she unpinned the Girl from the wall.

It took him five minutes to brew the tea. He made it strong and sweet and poured it into two earthenware mugs. When he came into the living-room she was standing by the table, his shirts over her arm.

"I'm sorry"—her voice was barely audible—"but I had to do it—for your sake."

Did executioners feel as she did, she wondered? She reminded herself that she had destroyed a photograph, not a living being. But she couldn't believe it.

The pieces were on the table—she had been particularly careful to tear the eyes into tiny fragments.

And then she looked at Lowell, suddenly afraid. He had a mug of tea in each hand and he kept holding them very steadily—or were they holding him, handcuffing him from violence? He dropped one and the hot liquid splashed on the floor, and then he let the other go and it cracked against the table and splintered. He picked up one of the shards and held it, his hand clawlike and rigid with anger.

She realised that he was capable of killing her. That if she didn't leave here quickly he would.

Clumsy with terror she stumbled towards the door.

FIVE

It was the flare-up of the arthritis that forced Lowell to go and see Ben. He parked his van in the grounds of the health centre and then went through the proper procedure at the reception desk. The receptionist, remembering him from last time when he had jumped the queue, told him that Dr. Sprackman was busy, but he might just manage to give him an end-of-morning appointment. She would phone through and see.

"He'll give it," Lowell said and rested his hands on the ledge by the receptionist's window. She noticed them. All patients here were sick in varying degrees, and this man's need was no greater than anyone else's, she reasoned. So she was surprised when the doctor said he would see him immediately.

"What the hell has been happening?" Ben asked when Lowell was shown in.

It was over a fortnight now since Zoe had returned from her visit to the cottage. When she and Lowell had failed to turn up for the dinner, Louise had gone to find out what was wrong. The back door had been open and she had found Zoe in the sitting-room gazing at a television quiz show, obviously not hearing it or seeing it. There had been stains on her skirt. The story she had given Louise had been garbled, something about a torn photograph and smashed mugs of tea. "And a lot more than that must have happened," Louise had told Ben. "She's shocked—I mean, almost clinically."

"Happening?" Lowell took the chair by the desk. "Nothing that need concern anyone—except you, in your professional capacity. Look."

His coldness stemmed from despair. The mental image of murder was sickeningly real, but couldn't be expressed. Peterson was alive. Zoe was alive. For that he was thankful. Let Ben cure what he might, or might not, be capable of curing—a flare-up of arthritis. The rest he'd have to cope with alone.

Ben, surprised and a little huffed to be put on the other side of the fence, felt the swollen joints and asked when the trouble had started.

"A couple of weeks ago."

About the time of the bother with Zoe, Ben thought. Probably a coincidence. But possibly not.

"Why didn't you come and see me earlier—at home?"

"I thought it would pass. And your home is too near mine."

"Meaning?"

"I don't want to see Zoe—either casually or intentionally."

"Why not?"

Because I'm afraid of my reaction, and if I tell you that, you'll want me to elaborate, and if I do you won't believe it.

He was silent.

"All families have rows," Ben said predictably. "Louise and I have occasionally hurled things at each other—well, she did the hurling. Nerves get tight. She loves the kids, but there are times when she finds them a strain. And then I get home a bit whacked and uptight from the hassles of the practice and we rub each other raw. And then there's a row. We usually make it up in bed. Sex is a great panacea."

Ben remembered what Louise had said about Zoe's frigidity. A guess, of course, but she could be right. Perhaps sex was the cause rather than the cure in this case. And how normal was Lowell's sexual drive?

He decided to move on to safer ground. "Your wife tells me you're working on a musical composition." Zoe's very precise description, voiced as an excuse for Lowell's absence, was clear in his mind.

"I was." Since the Girl had been destroyed he had pushed the manuscript away and couldn't bear to look at it. The nocturne had been for her. Now the nights were black and hideous with insomnia. She no longer spoke to him in his mind. He no longer dreamed of her. The exorcism was complete.

The past tense didn't surprise Ben. With distorted painful joints it would be difficult to hold a pen. He told him he'd give him tablets and wrote out the prescription. "You've had them before and they've worked. If they don't this time, I'll give you something else. It's the pattern of the illness to have periods of remission and relapse."

He then gave Lowell a general checkover and didn't discover anything new apart from the fact that he had lost a little weight. He warned him to eat properly, but refrained from telling him to go home where food could be cooked in a modern kitchen by a wife who had looked after him since their wedding day. It didn't occur to him to ask if he was drinking more than usual. Like that of many doctors, Ben's alcoholic intake was high. Higher than Lowell's. That the position was now reversed would have surprised him.

It was difficult to let an old friend walk out of the surgery after failing to make any sort of personal contact, and at the risk of blundering into a sensitive area he had to voice it: "Both Louise and I are worried about you and

Zoe. If there's anything we can do to help we'll gladly do it."

Lowell avoided looking at him and stared instead at the yellow trellised wallpaper. It was inappropriate in a doctor's surgery. So, too, were Ben's casual grey flannel suit and red tie. The sense of cosiness was false and he felt uncomfortable here. A professional visit should take place in an anonymous white cell of a room presided over by a stranger in a white coat, he decided. Open-heart surgery should be conducted decently in the right place, and with the patient's consent.

He replied stiffly that he and Zoe were managing their affairs—adequately. And then muttered a polite "Thank you for being concerned."

Ben reminded him to have the tablets made up. "And when you've finished them come and see me. Or, if necessary, I'll come out to the cottage."

He had intended asking him if he had a message for Zoe, but decided not to. Lowell had already distanced himself like a stranger departing over a hill.

Ben tried to explain it to Louise afterwards. "He stood at the door, just before leaving, and looked at me as if he hardly knew me. He had come for his tablets—and got them—and that was it. My work-load wasn't heavy, I could have suggested a pub lunch, but I didn't. He wouldn't have wanted me to. Excuses would have been embarrassing for both of us. Apart from the flare-up of the arthritis, I can't think what the hell's the matter with him. But something is."

"And with Zoe," Louise said. "She doesn't want him home any more." She hesitated. "And I don't think it's for any stupid reason, like hurt pride—I think she's afraid of him."

On the way back to the cottage Lowell stopped at an off-licence and bought a couple of bottles of scotch. He in-

tended to get plastered. The off-licence—which also dou-
bled as a grocery store—sold bread. He hadn't eaten fresh
bread for some time and chose a couple of crisp, well-
done loaves, though he didn't believe that acknowledging
a need to eat was a sign of healing. In the old days con-
demned prisoners ate breakfast before mounting the scaf-
fold. Nature nudged you into a habit.

The cottage, despite the loss of the Girl, still lured him.
It was a familiar lair. He didn't want to be anywhere else.
He was rational enough to know that he was in a deep
state of depression—and that the cause wouldn't stand
scrutiny. The Girl, in the ever-rational view of the outside world, was only a dead woman's fading image. He
had lost a piece of cardboard translated into a dream,
nothing more. He had killed his wife—inside his head—
nothing more. So climb out of your pit and rejoice.
There's nothing wrong. All is trivial.

He poured himself a liberal amount of neat whisky,
intending to drink to the fact.

And kept on drinking for a long time.

During the night the Charolais bull got loose and lumbered its heavy way across the fields. It impregnated a
Jersey cow from a neighbouring herd—an animal too
small to safely bear a calf by it—and then went on to
plunder the cottage garden. Lowell, awakened at some
time after three, heard a beast bellow and believed he'd
imagined it. The tablets and the booze were giving him
the best sleep he'd had for a long time and he needed
more. He pulled the pillow over his head, turned on his
side, and relaxed into darkness again.

Meanwhile the bull roamed on until captured by a couple of farm-hands later in the morning.

It was a bad case of negligence.

Craddock, the stockman, knew it. And so did Rose Ballater, the farmer's granddaughter. They stood locked in confrontation in the farmyard.

"It's your bull," Craddock said irritably. "You tell the colonel."

"It's your job to secure the animal at night," Rose pointed out. "I just lead him to the field occasionally."

"Like a damned poodle," Craddock expostulated.

"As curly-haired and as docile," Rose agreed, "but there the resemblance ends."

Craddock didn't believe the creature was docile. It responded to this frail-looking seventeen-year-old girl in some strange way, but not to him. He treated it warily and with respect.

"We'll split our responsibility," Rose suggested. "You'll tell Grandfather about the heifer—or heifers—a delicate subject. I'll tell Marshall about the wall."

Craddock amused her as much as she irritated him. He was small, bandy-legged, and not far off her grandfather in age. He wore striped collarless shirts of the old-fashioned kind and drill cotton breeches. He wiped his nose frequently on a khaki-coloured handkerchief that looked like army issue. In the distant past he had been batman to her grandfather and used the military title out of habit.

Now, tired and cross after trailing the animal, he looked at the girl with intense dislike. He was loath to take orders from her. Her bull had rampaged and she had blamed him. Her grandfather would blame him. He thought the situation over and had to concede that they might both be right. The bull was her pet—a dangerous one—but his responsibility.

"Very well," he said shortly.

She watched him trudging across the yard to the farmhouse and then made her way down to the cottage. This meeting, she sensed, was inevitable. Even if the bull hadn't knocked down the wall, it would have happened.

On the several occasions when she had broken into the
cottage in Marshall's absence she had half expected him
to return and find her. At times she had been tempted to
stay and let him. But that would have been manipulative.
It was more than a game of dare—he had invaded a place
she loved.

He had chopped up the dismembered piano for firewood at last, she noticed. Bits of mahogany had been left
lying around for ages; now they were in neat burnable
strips. He had piled up the ivory keys like a heap of old
knuckle-bones by the shed under a coil of wire. According to village gossip, he had been a famous pianist in his
day. Now he was a killer of inferior instruments—a
vandaliser of Miss Marshall's piano. Surely it hadn't been
bad enough for demolition. True, the old woman had
never played it, but even so . . .

Lowell, unaware that he was about to have a visitor,
was standing in the lean-to morosely waiting for the kettle to boil. The damage to the wall by an outside force—
probably that malignant brute of a bull—was just further
proof that the guardianship of his cottage wouldn't be
easy. Everyone—represented by Zoe—and every creature
—represented by the bull—wanted him out. This morning there had been a rat in the kitchen and he was as
bothered by that as by the rampaging bull. How did you
deal with rats? By traps? By poison? The wall could be
rebuilt—only to be knocked down again? One rat could
be expedited—only to be followed by more? The soothing effect of a good night's rest was being ruined by the
encroaching problems of the morning.

He had just made himself a mug of instant coffee when
she knocked on his door. Annoyed by the intrusion, he
took a couple of sips of the hot liquid before going to
open it.

Rose had only seen Marshall at a distance, coming and

going in his yellow van. His appearance now, as he stood looking down at her, shocked her. She had imagined him different. Concert pianists were the smoothies of the world—they removed night-time stubble—or they presented morning beards sleekly combed. They were clean and unharassed. This man had the smashed, dazed look of an alcoholic.

It was some moments before either of them spoke and then they both spoke together. She began explaining about the bull and he asked her her name. In the jumble of sentences nothing made sense. They paused and silently looked at each other, Lowell still holding his coffee. His hands weren't long, slim and delicate. They were thick and red and trembled. She suddenly thought: Your poor hands . . . for God's sake . . . how awful for you.

He simply looked and couldn't believe what he saw. Her dark curly hair was worn loose over her shoulders— whereas the Girl's was scraped back. The sepia print hadn't revealed the reddish streaks at the temples—neither had it shown that the eyes were blue, a deep dark blue. The lips were the same—full, soft, gently curved. But the Girl's lips were amused. This girl's were not. This girl was younger. She hadn't yet grown into the skin of the older one. He pulled himself up sharply and chided himself for being too fanciful—or too booze-sodden—to think rationally. How could she grow into the skin of someone who was dead?

She was the first to regain a degree of composure. "I come from Ballater's farm—it's just over the hill. I'm Stuart Ballater's granddaughter. He'll pay for the damage— or one of the farm-hands will rebuild the wall."

So that was how She spoke, he thought. Rather clipped voice, pitched low. It was as he had imagined it. The kind of voice that could make music in your head, not rasp cruelly in your brain. Not a Zoe voice.

He again asked what her name was.

"Rose Ballater."

"Rose," he said, "of course." She looked at him, astonished. "It's perfect."

After a few moments' hesitation she started to explain about the bull again. "It's the first time he has broken loose . . ." But Lowell wasn't listening. He felt euphoric, as if he had walked out of a long dark tunnel into blazing sunlight. There was a mad kind of joy in this impossible landscape. Careful, he warned himself. Careful. If he didn't force his imagination to slink back into the greyness of the world as it was, he'd scare this perfectly ordinary twentieth-century girl—with a small *g*—away. Rose. A nice name that suited any century. Not unique.

But She had been Rose. Undoubtedly. And this Rose was talking to him now. "Shall we go and look at the damage so that I can tell my grandfather the extent of it?"

He had been about to ask her to step inside, but feared she might refuse. She was like a bird alighting too close. Give her space. Give her time. Use the soft pedal—there's too much loud music in your head. Quieten everything. Be calm.

She walked ahead of him into the garden and he looked at her from behind. A view of Rose that the picture couldn't have given him. She wore a dark blue sweatshirt and pale blue denim shorts frayed at the edges. Neat waist. Legs lightly tanned. Open sandals. Scarlet varnish beginning to chip on toenails. None of the sartorial elegance of the photograph.

She picked her way carefully through the wild garden made wilder by the scattered stones from the wall. Hoof prints showed clearly in the soil, proof of the huge size of the animal. A clump of feverfew, uprooted and drying in the morning sun, lay on a bed of mint. A gentle embracing in a scene of havoc.

She said, "I'm not an expert—but this sort of dry stonewalling should be put right without too much bother. It's lucky you hadn't done any planting here."

A prosaic assessment.

He forced himself to see everything her way—an ordinary way—and went to examine the wall, mainly to prevent her looking too closely at him. It was usually possible to mouth the right words, but the eyes spoke differently.

He picked up a large stone and put it near the base of the broken wall. This was the area where he had found the piece of urn. Given time, and more digging around, he might find more. He told her he thought he could rebuild it himself.

"But why should you? César is my bull. My responsibility."

Her bull? An odd possession for a girl so frail. Surprise in this context was natural; he turned and looked at her. *"Your* bull?"

"Part of the farm livestock, of course. But I saw it arrive in the world. It thinks it's mine, and I haven't disillusioned it."

It might be safer, he thought, if she had.

"It's the farm's liability," she persisted. "And in any case how could you do that sort of rough work with your hands?"

He had forgotten that his hands pained him. The nerve cells, suddenly prodded into remembering, began to throb again. He clenched his fists and put them behind his back. They were unpleasant, off-putting hands. He wished she hadn't seen them.

"The old woman who used to live here grew herbs," she said. "Feverfew is good for rheumatism." She pointed at the uprooted clump. "I remember some of the villagers coming here for it."

"The old woman? You mean Miss Marshall?"

"Yes. Was she a relative?"

"A cousin many times removed. I didn't know her."
This was conversation for conversation's sake. For both
of them. They were studying each other, and she, aware
of his controlled excitement, was disturbed by it. He,
aware of her awareness, took a few paces away from her.
He picked a leaf of the feverfew, "This stuff?"

"Yes—as far as I know it didn't poison anyone."

"Or cure them?"

"I wouldn't know."

"But you knew Miss Marshall?"

"When I came here first as a child—with my parents—
to stay with my grandfather—I used to escape down here.
I was about nine at the time."

"Escape?"

She had used the word lightly; now she was forced to
think about it. "From oppressive, dominating people.
Missy didn't bother me. She let me roam around."

There was a small cleft in her chin—almost a dimple.
He tried to remember if the Girl—the other Rose—had
one too.

"Missy," she said, aware of his scrutiny and fending
him away with words, "was the villagers' name for Miss
Marshall. I don't know why. It didn't suit her. She was
tall, gaunt, about seventy and always wore an old red
dressing-gown over a black woollen dress—a bit scary-
looking until you got used to her. When they came for
her herb cures I used to slip out through the back. I didn't
want my family to know I visited her—the villagers
might tell them. She had an odd reputation. I didn't know
that then. I just knew she was different. And I liked her
as she was."

"And you liked the cottage."

It wasn't a question. She wondered how he knew.

"You either like it—a lot—or you loathe it. There's nothing in between. I can't explain it. Nobody can."

Lowell asked her if she were holidaying on the farm now. She explained that her grandfather had become her legal guardian when her parents died. "I help around the place generally."

"You're not planning a career?"

"Academically, I'm a disaster. But I like animals. A farm is a preparation for an abattoir—that bothers me. I dare to love my bull. No farmer, especially my grandfather, will kill off a randy Charolais. César is safe while he screws."

Lowell felt as if he had reached out to touch a familiar hand and recoiled from a stranger's. He remembered the amused eyes in the photograph. The idea might have occurred to Her, but she wouldn't have voiced it that way.

The dream had to be adjusted—or rejected.

She said, "I've shocked you." And now the amusement was clear in her eyes, too.

He denied it.

She became practical again. "Do I send one of the farmhands down to rebuild the wall?"

He suggested leaving it for a few days. He'd have a go at putting it together himself. And if he didn't get on too well with it, either because he hadn't the expertise, or his hands proved a nuisance, then someone else could take over.

She asked if he was positive he wanted to try and he replied it would be therapeutic.

Emotional therapy, she thought. Something is bugging him. *I'm* bugging him. I wonder why? The knowledge intrigued her.

She suggested calling again at midweek. "To see how you're managing. And don't struggle with it. You don't have to do it all."

And you didn't have to make the assignation, Lowell

thought. You could send someone else along, but you won't. Happiness began bubbling in him again, almost beyond control. Whoever she was, he wanted to know her. And she, obviously, wanted to know him.

SIX

"You take too much on yourself," Ballater told his grand-daughter. "If I want you to act as my emissary, I shall tell you so. And stop antagonising Craddock. It's not your place to give him orders."

It was lunch-time. An hour after Rose had returned from the cottage. The meal was laid in the large, cold, timber-ceilinged dining-room, a joyless room filled with oil paintings of rural scenes yellowed by age. Ballater fitted the environment. He wouldn't have described himself as landed gentry—or if he did it would be with irony. He had retired early as lieutenant-colonel on inheriting the farm and wished the local people would drop the title. Craddock was the most persistent user. "We're both civilians," he had told him crisply when he first took him on. "Any warring we do here is with the Ministry of Agriculture." And although Craddock's warring with his grand-daughter was usually out of earshot and not spoken of, today he had complained.

Rose shrugged. To argue with the old man was pointless. These mealtime confrontations always took the edge off her appetite. She would have preferred to eat in the kitchen at the large scrubbed table with the farm-hands and Mrs. Hopkins, the housekeeper. This sort of segregation was feudal.

She passed her grandfather the courgettes. The vegetables, not well cooked, lay hard but neat in the Crown Derby dish. He declined them.

"Sensible," she said, trying to turn the subject. "The only edible concoction Mrs. Hopkins can produce is stew."

Too late she realised that she had let her defences down. Now he would invite her to do better—after a course of Cordon Bleu cookery, perhaps.

He resisted the temptation. She was idle, at times insolent, and rarely co-operative. Always a worry. If past events could be regarded more calmly he would handle her better. He knew this and tried, though never successfully. That he had a deep affection for her no one knew, certainly not Rose. He had always hidden his feelings admirably.

"What's Marshall like?" he asked.

She wasn't sure how to answer. A physical description was easier than an emotional assessment. If you were groggy on speed you behaved a bit like Marshall—your feet weren't solidly stuck to the ground—there was a look in your eyes that wasn't lust—and wasn't all purity, either—amazed recognition summed it up, but didn't make sense.

"Tall, dark, rather ill-looking," she said finally.

"Is his arthritis obvious?"

She was surprised. "How did you know about it?"

"My dear girl, I may be moronic as far as modern music is concerned, but I have attended classical concerts in my time. I haven't seen Marshall perform, but I've heard his records. He had remarkable talent. His reason for quitting made news."

"His hands are swollen, yes," Rose said.

"Then what's all this nonsense about rebuilding a wall?"

"It's what he wants to do."

Ballater looked at his granddaughter with quite unjustified irritation. What had she said to Marshall, he wondered, to needle him into such a ridiculous response? He asked her.

Rose pushed her plate aside. She tried to speak levelly and control her temper. "We had a normal conversation. I wasn't aggressive. Neither was he. He's doing what he wants to do. That's all."

"So you keep saying." And perhaps correctly, he thought. Marshall's hands had once made music—now they couldn't—so he was perhaps punishing them with hard labour in a sort of brutal compensation. It was either that, or she had upset him. He decided to go down to the cottage during the afternoon and find out for himself.

It didn't take Lowell long to realise that the bull hadn't unearthed any pieces of urn. His disappointment was mild. The urn represented a bridge with the past, but a careful piecing together of shards to make the bridge perfect wasn't necessary. Rose had walked it. Or he thought she had. Two voices spoke to him in his head. The first told him he was irrational, that the obsession was dangerous. The second told him to question nothing. To wait passively and accept.

He felt good. Even his hands were better. But they weren't capable hands. He was carefully trying to place one stone on top of another when Ballater called on him.

"It's not as easy as it might appear," Ballater commented, and then introduced himself.

Lowell, thrust into the present day and onto solid ground, agreed that he wasn't much good at it.

A light rain began to fall, drawing up a sharp smell of weeds and grasses. Ballater, advancing into the garden, noticed a heap of uprooted dead cannabis tangled with chickweed on the small cleared area. He was both startled and dismayed. Obviously it hadn't been planted by Marshall; the weed was the remains of a previous year's crop.

Lowell, aware that his visitor's attention was deflected from him and onto the compost heap, was puzzled. The old man was wearing a plastic raincoat but was hatless. His bald head filmed with rain.

He invited him to come into the cottage out of the wet.

Ballater appeared not to hear him. "You'd better burn that"—he indicated the compost—"or bury it. It's fortunate the police haven't found it."

Lowell was puzzled. "Found what?"

"Cannabis. Tinkers were camped in the field just across the wall last year." A lie went against the grain, but was necessary. "The old woman's garden was convenient, or at least her fertile cabbage patch. It's the only explanation I can think of—no one else would plant it."

Lowell remembered the pungent smell in the cottage. He had recognised that, but not the leaf. He told Ballater that someone had been breaking in. "The fire has been lit and allowed to die down a couple of times—and I once smelt the stuff."

Ballater looked at him sharply. "You're sure?"

"Oh, yes. The last time was two or three weeks ago. The intruder, whoever it was, seems to see the cottage as home from home."

He could sense that the old man was deeply troubled. For his part, he wasn't too bothered. It was disconcerting, nothing more. Illegal seeds had been sown in the cabbage patch when the cottage was empty. They wouldn't be sown again. "I'll get rid of it," he told Ballater. "And get the lock on my back door fixed. That should be the end of the matter."

He suggested again that they should retreat inside before they got wetter.

The last time Ballater had been in the cottage was just before Miss Marshall had been forced out of it by her rapacious relatives, backed up by the insensitive local general practitioner, who agreed she couldn't cope. Ballater had, on that visit, thought the place loathsome—it still was—but he had felt a degree of sympathy with her for wanting to stay. The middle-aged tended to become power-happy if they had geriatrics in the family. They uprooted them, as Marshall had uprooted the cannabis, and watched them wither.

He had intended making an offer for the cottage, but the old woman's distress at leaving had made him change his mind. She hadn't been sufficiently strong mentally, he believed, to will the money away from her destroyers. He had been wrong. Marshall, according to some discreet enquiries he had made, was innocent of trespass—of any kind.

So the time to buy the place could be now. He broached the matter carefully while Marshall put a match to some logs in the grate. The flames curled slowly, sending flickers of light onto the walls. The cottage, he told Marshall, had been built the same time as the farm. The Ballaters, in those days, owned it. Later it was sold. He didn't tell him why. These days the property itself had no value unless you happened to have a farm over the hill. A second means of access would be possible if the cottage were gutted. The geological nature of the land precluded access from any other part of his property. A track wide enough for a tractor could be taken down to the road. Useful in a bad winter. Snow tended to pile up and block access to the road on the other side.

Lowell sat back on his heels and watched the flames. This man wanted to buy his cottage and demolish it. The idea was so outrageous it was unbelievable.

Ballater, too keen a businessman to throw his money around, proceeded to try to persuade Marshall into a satisfactory deal. "One has to be realistic about these places. I imagine you came here with the intention of doing it up

and then realised the enormous extent of the work
needed to put it right." He looked around the room. Obviously Marshall, apart from daubing one of the walls
and putting up a piece of corkboard, hadn't done anything. "If you want to sell and get as far as enticing a
buyer, whoever it is will have the place surveyed, and
any surveyor knowing his job will condemn it out of
hand. It hasn't even any so-called old world charm, and
the site is too low to command a good view."

Marshall's continuing silence was beginning to bother
him. "Well," he prompted, "wouldn't you agree?"

Lowell stood up. He needed a drink. Politeness forced
him to offer one. "Whisky?"

"What? No. I mean, thank you, but I don't indulge.
Coffee, perhaps, or tea?"

Oh, Christ, Lowell thought. He went out to the lean-to
to make it. The mug he had used in the morning was still
unwashed and his two spare mugs had been smashed
during Zoe's last visit. That time it had been tea. This
time he made coffee in cups and put whisky in his. This
time he wasn't so angry. Rose's grandfather had made a
stupid suggestion but he had also thrown some light on
the history of the cottage. It was interesting that it had
once belonged to the Ballaters. The Rose of the photograph might have been Rose's great-grandmother, perhaps. It would account for the strong resemblance. He
was tempted to ask Ballater about it and then decided not
to. It would be unwise, he guessed, to speak of Rose to
the old man. And he no longer had the photograph.

Ballater was crouching in front of the fire warming his
hands when Lowell returned. There were brown age
marks on them like a scattering of large freckles. But they
looked supple, nevertheless.

"It's extremely difficult to heat this sort of place in the
winter," he continued, taking the coffee from Lowell.
"The only kind of central heating possible would be solid

fuel and to install it would cost more than the cottage is worth." The offering price he had in mind was four thousand pounds. He would have given more to the old woman, but Marshall, despite the way he looked, was probably well heeled.

"I use logs," Lowell said. He hadn't thought about the winter yet. The winter didn't matter.

Ballater sensed obstinate refusal rather than a willingness to bargain. He wondered what Marshall's wife thought about it. "Had you and Mrs. Marshall planned to use it as a weekend retreat, perhaps? Surely, if you had, you would have discovered the drawbacks by now?"

Lowell had no intention of discussing Zoe. He was glad she wasn't there to listen. Off-load it, she would tell him. Let the abominable place go.

"The drawbacks," he said, "I can cope with."

Ballater reassessed his offer in the face of resistance. "I'd take it off your hands for four and a half thousand."

Lowell smiled. "The price of your Charolais bull?"

Ballater couldn't see any connection. Anyway, the bull was worth more. Quite a bit more. But this man wasn't haggling with him. The musician, for some reason he couldn't understand, didn't want to sell. So don't press him. Wait. The winter would force him out.

"The bull is a valuable asset," he said smoothly, "and only occasionally a liability. If you should find the cottage more a liability than you had envisaged then we can perhaps talk business in the future. In the meantime I'll make sure that the bull doesn't make a nuisance of itself again—and I'll get the wall rebuilt." A thought struck him. "Get rid of the cannabis before my men come. They're unlikely to recognise it—presumably you didn't —but you can't take chances."

Lowell said he'd dig it in. He was aware that Ballater was looking at his hands and assured him that he could wield a spade perfectly well.

Ballater, in the last few minutes of his visit, praised his performance as a pianist and the atmosphere became more cordial. The old man was knowledgeable about music. It didn't occur to Lowell to wonder how he had also familiarised himself with drugs.

Back at the farm Ballater called Rose into his study. It was a summons, not a request. A court martial rather than a discussion. He accused her of planting the cannabis. She denied it. He accused her of smoking it in Marshall's cottage. She denied that, too. He threatened to hand her over to the police if she had any more of it. She spoke truthfully for the first time and said she hadn't any more of it—which was a direct admission that she had had it in the first place.

He despaired of her and wished to God she wasn't his responsibility. The generation gap here was too wide. She was, he supposed, typical of her contemporaries. She hadn't been the only one to be quietly expelled from the eminently respectable boarding school after being caught smoking cannabis. What was the matter with the young of these days that they were in such haste to destroy themselves? Was their inheritance that bad? He thought of Rose's lineage, where the power to hurt—and be hurt—was strong.

She was waiting for him to rant on—her face coolly patient. He could tell by her eyes that she had closed her mind to him. As she had learnt to do. Communication was impossible. He was no good with soft words, gentle phrases. But she was his son's child and he cared for her. He wished she could understand that without having to be told.

"Leave Marshall alone," he warned. "Any business that needs to be done with him, I'll see to."

"The musician," she replied, and with a degree of amusement in her voice, "is of no interest to me."

. . . .

On the morning the men came to rebuild the wall, Lowell was still in bed. Rose, ignoring her grandfather's orders, came briefly to watch them. Lowell, hearing her voice through the bedroom window, dressed hastily and splashed his face with cold water, but by this time she had gone. It was ten-thirty. His backsliding into sloth had happened so slowly that he hadn't been aware of it. He looked at himself critically in the small mirror on the window ledge in the lean-to. No wonder she hadn't stayed. He needed sprucing up. A haircut—a decent shave. And the cottage was filthy.

His upward swing of mood since meeting Rose was like a glider flying above the clouds where all was serene. He was quite sure she would visit him again. And when she did the cottage would have a shine on it. No cobwebs in corners. No linen that wasn't sweet. No rat droppings under the sink.

He needed to do some shopping for cleaning materials and other basic necessities and decided to go to Cheltenham. The van was reluctant to start but he coaxed it patiently. A few days ago an uncooperative van would have sent him back indoors in a state of deep despair. Had his depression lasted much longer he would have become agoraphobic. Until Rose came he had reached the stage of not wanting to go out. Everything out here—the fast road —the wide fields—the sweep of the sky—had been oppressive and inimical. Today it was stimulating. Pleasant. His hands were much better and could grip the steering wheel without pain. He felt rested. Last night he had slept well—too well.

Next time she came . . .

He began fantasising and had to take avoiding action when he took a corner too wide. The outside world needed his undivided attention. Today it was complicated, but not menacing. The vibes generally were good.

He even managed to park near the centre of the town without trouble. People were helpful, too. Kindly. Nice. The woman in the launderette showed him where to put the coins. The ironmonger explained how the mousetrap should be set. The trappings of death, he'd joked. Not funny, but he'd smiled politely. It occurred to him after he'd bought the cleaning materials and collected his laundry that his shirts would need ironing. He hadn't an iron. He went into one of the large stores and bought one, and then remembered there was no electricity in the cottage. He was exasperated, but not cast down. The shop assistant laughed with him and gave him his money back. Drip-dry shirts were the answer, she said. He thought he probably had them already, but bought three more in case he hadn't. Immaculate cuffs and collars were Zoe's department. He remembered her at moments such as these and felt a twinge of guilt—not a searing kick in the gut—which, he supposed, was something else to be thankful for.

Before leaving town he had a professional shave, shampoo and trim—not too much off—just the straggle of hair over his collar. His appearance was rather more conformist now—he looked more like the Lowell of the old days.

And Rose looked like . . . Rose. He saw her face clearly, sometimes in the photograph, sometimes in the flesh. And he didn't have to drink to see it. At least, not much. A drop of scotch during occasional periods of self-criticism helped him to become happy with himself, but most of the time he was happy anyway.

Since Rose had come.

She visited him two days later, just after he had cut his thumb on the mousetrap and was bleeding into the sink. Had he arranged it, he couldn't have planned it better. She had been uneasy about the visit; the cottage, as always, drew her, despite the fact that she wasn't sure of Marshall. But a man who bled was vulnerable, and a wound caused by a mousetrap showed a reassuring degree of incompetence.

She examined the cut. "It's not deep. Where's your first-aid box?"

He hadn't one.

"Cotton wool," she suggested, "or lint?"

He hadn't any of those either.

She smiled. He was helpless, hopeless, reassuringly normal. What had she seen in him the other day that had been so disturbing?

He told her to look in the table drawer in the living room—he thought there might be a spare drying-up cloth in it. There was. It was blue. She warned him that the dye might come out and that he'd get blood poisoning. He said he'd probably get it anyway, that he'd baited the trap with a piece of meat that had gone off. Cheese, she told him, was more usual. "But you haven't any," she mimicked, and gently and competently dealt with the wound.

He thanked her and didn't know what else to say. Nor did she. Her fingers after bandaging his were stained with his blood. She dipped them in the washing-up bowl and dried them on the towel behind the door. He muttered something about the place being primitive. But clean, she thought; you've worked at it. And at yourself.

She observed that he had a funny-looking bath. "It's the sort of thing Miss Marshall would have kept coal in."

"I'm not reduced to that." But I'm reduced to verbal inanities, he thought. This is a non-conversation. This is ridiculous. You smell of clover fields. Do you know how lovely you are?

She was aware that his attention was focussing too strongly and too disconcertingly on her again. She said she couldn't stay, that she had just dropped in for a minute. "The village shop sells first-aid stuff. And if you'll take my advice you'll throw that trap away. What you need here is a cat. I'll get you one."

She went swiftly over to the door and had gone before he could answer.

SEVEN

Ben and Louise drove to the cottage on a Saturday afternoon. Ben could think of better ways of spending his free day—a round of golf—even doing the garden—but according to Louise, and he had to agree with her, you didn't ditch a friend because a friend ditched you. Lowell and Zoe were in a deadlocked situation—neither would budge. "So it's up to us to heal the breach," Louise urged. Ben wasn't so sure of the wisdom of positive action; it could be taken as interference. But Louise had already thought of that. "His hands need looking at," she reminded him. "It must be nearly a month since he called at the surgery. He'll be out of tablets by now. You can be calling professionally. As for me—well, I'm just coming for the ride."

It was an acrimonious ride, during which they had an argument about Lowell's sustenance and bedding. Louise had baked a pie for him and was bringing a new pair of sheets from the airing cupboard. Zoe had opted out of all domestic commitments. She wouldn't go with them. She had no message. Yes, she agreed with Louise, quarrels could be mended by talking. Most quarrels. But not theirs. She thought Lowell was sick in his head. Her parting shot had been to warn them not to bring back his dirty washing.

"If anyone is sick mentally," Louise stormed as they drove away from her, "it's Zoe. Damn it, they had a row. A bad one. She needled him too much and punctured his control. He scared her. But he didn't touch her. And now what is she doing? Spending like hell. She spilt tea on her suit—and what does she do? Have it cleaned? Oh, no. She buys another equally expensive model. *More* expensive. Is that rational behavior? She goes from one extreme to the other. Parsimonious when he leaves his job—to make him feel guilty. And now it's spend—spend— spend. Of course I've made him a pie—why shouldn't I? She won't. But if it helps to get them together I'll say she made it. And if he hasn't changed his sheets by now, he jolly well ought to have done. And I'll wash the others for him."

Ben forbade her to do any such thing. Zoe had made her statement of intent—a withdrawal of domestic support. Louise was to mind her own business and not queer the pitch. Metaphors became mixed and feelings ran high. In the end he capitulated to the extent of offering to hand over the sheets himself, but refused to say they were Zoe's. The hazards of becoming embroiled in domestic squabbles—and he still saw this as one—were their repercussions. Louise at the height of their row had called him a shit.

It was difficult to remember the route, but Lowell's van in the bottom field signposted them in the right direction. Without it they might have driven past the track and searched on fruitlessly. Ben parked his newly acquired BMW at the roadside and hoped it would be there when he returned, reassuring himself that in this place of utter solitude car thieves weren't likely to creep out of the hedgerows with duplicate keys.

Louise walked ahead of him up the path, carrying the pie in a wicker basket. He followed with the sheets in a blue plastic bag. When they reached the cottage they both felt the need for unity. Although the sun shone on its ancient walls, it looked cold and forbidding.

"The anchorite's cell," Ben muttered.

"Be kind," Louise warned him.

Lowell, hoping it was Rose, let his disappointment show. But he masked it quickly and invited them in. Louise kissed him and gave him the pie. She didn't say she had made it. Ben told him that she had. He got rid of the sheets by putting them on a chair near the passageway to the bedroom. With luck they wouldn't be remarked upon.

They all sat down.

Lowell told them politely and falsely that it was good to see them. These were his friends but he felt unnatural in their company, as if he were acting a part. Louise, his warm-hearted, likeable former neighbour, was looking at him with obvious concern. He wondered why.

If he had asked her she couldn't have answered. No one was ringing a mourning bell here. Lowell, a little thinner than usual, looked well enough. He had an air of self-containment, bordering on contentment. But he wasn't the Lowell she had known. Ben had mentioned his withdrawal and she hadn't taken him too seriously. Now she did. Here in this macabre place, away from everyone, he had found affinity. He hadn't wanted them to come and disturb his peace, that was obvious. There was no ease in the relationship any more; he saw them as strangers. She remembered with sadness all the neighbourly contacts they had had in the past—Lowell's anxiety when Edward had gone missing on his new bike during a November fog and his tireless search until he was found—his ham-fisted efforts to assist her in Ben's absence when the washing-machine had flooded the kitchen—his quiet piano playing, when his hands were still capable, at the end of a noisy party when all the guests had gone home. Lowell's humour—unexpected—that could take the heat

out of a fraught situation. His edginess and irritable out-
bursts that could put it back in. Lowell—very volatile—
her one-time good friend.

Ben, less concerned with Lowell's psyche than with his
physical well-being, examined his hands. They were better, showing hardly any inflammation now. He noticed,
however, that he had cut his thumb and that the edges of
the wound had been slow to heal. "You could have done
with a couple of stitches here. What happened?"

Lowell told him about the trap. "I wasn't much good at
setting it."

"You know how clumsy you are with anything me-
chanical—you'd be safer with a colony of rodents."

Louise shuddered. "Why don't you get *out* of this
place?"

It was a Zoe question. He wondered if Zoe had sent her
to ask it. "I'm never getting out of it." He spoke with
emphasis and with complete conviction.

Louise looked across at Ben. His eyes warned her to
shut up, not to probe further. She ignored him.

"What about Zoe?"

"What about her?"

"Do you expect her to join you here?"

"No."

"Do you intend going home to explain all this to her
soon?"

He was silent.

"Well—do you?"

Ben intervened. "Leave it! This is Lowell's affair, not
ours." Smiling awkwardly, he cast around for a topic of
conversation that wasn't personal and had difficulty in
finding one. It was too soon to leave, the atmosphere was
too tense, and it would have to become calm again or to
revisit wouldn't be possible. For Zoe's sake it might be
necessary for them to come back. They were a link—if at
the moment, a tenuous one.

From where he was sitting by the narrow little window he had a view of the meagre garden and beyond it, in the distance, a huge white bull in a field of white heifers. "A dangerous-looking animal," he commented.

Lowell went over to the window, mainly to get away from Louise's accusing eyes. "It's safe in its own field. It doesn't break out and go on the rampage when it's there." He explained about the garden wall and then went on to speak of Ballater's visit. "He wants to buy the property. I'm not selling."

"And do we tell Zoe that?" Louise asked.

Lowell shrugged. "Whether you tell her or not makes no difference."

They stayed an hour—an endurance test for tact. Louise, gritting her teeth against saying everything she wanted to say, spent part of the time making tea in the terrible little lean-to. She had to concede it was clean. There was bread and butter, both fresh, and an assortment of tinned food. On the physical level, at least, he wasn't letting himself go.

They were taking their leave when they saw Rose walking down the field path. She saw them at the same moment and hesitated, then she turned and began walking back the way she had come. "A young girl, long dark hair, ordinary looking," Louise described her to Zoe later. "She was carrying a kitten." She didn't describe Lowell's expression as he watched her go, nor the speed with which he'd followed her after he had abruptly said good-bye to them.

"So that's how it is," Ben said when they reached the car. He was both astonished and amused.

She told him he was jumping to conclusions.

Miss Marshall's black cat, according to Rose, had been called Midnight—like this one—Middy for short. He could change the name if he wanted to. He didn't. Mid-

night, according to one's mood, conjured up romantic or
macabre visions. In his present happy state the former
applied, but he was careful to keep his feelings in check.
The relationship that had been started by the bull was
being carried on very satisfactorily by the comings and
goings of the kitten. It regularly returned to the farm and
was regularly brought back by Rose. Her confidence grew
at each visit.

Today she wanted to know about his visitors.

Just friends, he told her.

"Doesn't your wife visit any more?"

"No." He didn't elaborate.

If he wanted to be cagey, she thought, that was okay
by her. The wife—temporarily—was off the scene. Good.
She went to sit on the floor where the rush matting was
covered by a rug and rested her back against the sofa. The
kitten clung to her shoulder, its small sharp teeth pulling
at strands of her hair. She lifted it away and put it on
Lowell's knee. It didn't want to stay there and came
bounding back to her.

He leaned over and stroked it. "He will always follow
you back to the farm."

"Have you tried putting butter on his feet?"

"Yes, he licked it off, and then followed you back."

"What are you feeding him on? Scraps?"

"No—tinned stuff from the village."

"God, what a waste! Dried milk too, I suppose? I'll
bring you down some fresh."

He was pleased she hadn't suggested that he should
fetch it. He didn't want to run into Ballater again; his
wish to purchase the cottage put him in the enemy camp
and threatened his peace. He and Rose were better meeting here, on their own, in their own place. That the cottage meant as much to her as it did to him was obvious,
but it didn't occur to him that she might have been the
intruder who had broken in. Had it not been for the smell

of pot he might have suspected it. He had told her about
the cannabis bed a few days ago when they had been
walking in the garden, and her eyes had widened in
shock. "By God!" she had said.

Despite what he saw as her sweetness—her innocence
—he sensed at times that physical contact wasn't just a
remote dream.

It had long stopped being a remote dream to Rose. Now
that Lowell had learnt to handle the relationship without
being too intense—and was drinking less—she was finding him physically attractive. A refreshing change from
her usual, inexperienced escorts.

But how to make her feelings plain?

Her grandfather, she remembered, had expressed his
feelings about Lowell very plainly indeed. Which for
Rose increased the appeal of forbidden fruit. Any man
with self-respect, he said, wouldn't tolerate such a
squalid environment. And the musician himself was as
seedy as his surroundings—unshaven and obviously
drinking too much. His coffee had stunk of whisky. He
needed his wife's presence to spruce him up and to take
both him and the cottage in hand.

Mention of Lowell's wife was, Rose knew, a repeated
and none too subtle warning for her to keep away from
him. That Lowell and the cottage had been spruced up
since her grandfather's visit—and in his wife's continuing
absence—was something she wasn't supposed to know. It
had been difficult to remain silent, but she had.

Coming here, clandestinely, added spice to the visits.

"I can stay a little while," she said. Very prim. Rather
ambiguous.

The kitten was cradled in her arms and she ran her
fingers gently up and down its stomach so that it purred
with delight. She looked at Lowell, her eyes narrowed so
that the sexual invitation wasn't too overt. She smiled.
Caressed. Sighed a little.

He was getting the message, but wasn't quite sure. She was seventeen. A child. The other one—the Girl—the other Rose—had excited him sexually. A dream woman. A photograph. Invulnerable.

The kitten was dribbling with pleasure. Rose's hand was small and freckled, and it teased and rubbed. All the while she watched him covertly, smiling. Her tongue touched the edge of her teeth, withdrew, appeared again.

He half turned from her. For God's sake, just how innocent was she?

She said, "What's this?"

It didn't matter to her what it was—a piece of stone on the hearth—just something to talk about—an embarrassed need for words to cover what she saw as his rejection.

When he turned to her again he saw that she had put the cat down and was holding the piece of urn. He felt both excited and claustrophobic, as if the cottage walls were closing in on him and then receding. He didn't know if he was back in time, or here in the present. He spoke her name quietly.

"It's all right," she said briskly, "I've done it before." This time there was no ambiguity.

He undressed her in the bedroom in a ritual of tenderness. Amused, she let him. Her scarlet T-shirt was innocent of graffiti and her jeans were neatly patched. Her pants, a wisp of white cotton, had an edging of lace. She had dressed with some care. Now, undressed, she stood on her discarded clothes. Her body, small, slim, was the colour of cream.

Lowell's love-making was both passionate and gentle. He cared about her pleasure and she responded to him more strongly then she had with anyone. Afterwards, sated and happy, they both slept while the afternoon sun crept into the room and lingered a while on the wall where the photograph had been. Lowell, the first to wake, saw the splash of yellow on the empty corkboard and thought he still dreamed. And then he felt Rose's warm body pressed up against his. This was reality, whatever that might mean. This was Rose—past, present and future.

She opened her eyes and smiled at him. "Let's do it again," she said.

In the weeks following his bedding of Rose, Lowell gave himself to her totally. Not only physically and emotionally—but intellectually. The nocturne began to grow again and the music was her essence. He wrote it with delight and despair. Delight because it brought her close to him when the cottage was empty—despair because his talent was in his hands rather than in his composing ability. He wished it were better and deplored the imperfections. That Rose herself was imperfect he refused to admit, refused even to contemplate, even though her lovemaking was surprisingly accomplished for one so young. When she was half asleep and off guard, her vocabulary was raunchy. The fact that for a lot of the time she was on guard disturbed him. She had opened her body to him, but not her mind. He wanted all of her.

Rose, within her careful limits, gave what she could, including a lot of make-believe. She created a background which was only in part true. Her father had died in a car accident, she told him. That he had been well over the limit, both speed and booze limits, following a blazing row with her mother, she had kept to herself. A sad description of her mother's death shortly afterwards—from grief—was perhaps stretching his credulity a bit, but she chanced it. Anyway, she wasn't sure of the facts. It had happened when she was away at school and her grandfather had glossed over the whole sorry business to the best of his ability. His one slip had been using the phrase "whole sorry business." "Sad loss" would have described heart failure—or whatever. And she hadn't died in her own bed. Extraordinarily embarrassing, Rose thought, for the owner of the bed. She had wept at the death of her father, but for her mother she felt no grief. The maternal bond had been cut with the umbilical cord—at birth. Her father had cuddled her when she was a child; all the loving in her childhood had come from him. Later, when she was in her early teens and beginning to look more like her mother, he had appeared to love her less. To win affection, she discovered, you had to project the sort of image the other person wanted, and you only did that if the image appealed to you and if the other person was worth the effort. Lowell, this strangely attractive, very intense man, was. The image was still nebulous; she couldn't quite see it, though the cottage helped. The acting she did within its framework was almost right. And occasionally she didn't even seem to be acting at all.

Out of the cottage, away from Lowell, she became herself again. Slanging matches with Craddock just for the hell of it. Cold, fairly polite, differences of opinion with her grandfather. Jokes with the younger farm-hands who were wise enough not to go too far with the granddaughter of the boss. Her quiet periods were spent walking on her own, avoiding useful jobs. Her grandfather had suggested, without conviction, that she might be of some use in the farm office. She had refused to disrupt an already smoothly running system and he hadn't pressed the point. The farm was her prison until her inheritance from her father's estate freed her in three years' time. Her grandfather's insistence that she was free to go out into the world now and take a course of training was so much nonsense. There was nothing she wanted to train for. Just as there was nothing Lowell wanted to devote himself to —other than music. And she had the edge on him because there was money to come. Money, obtained too easily, could finance disaster, her grandfather had warned

her; it must be used wisely when the time came. His idea
of wisdom and hers differed. It was wise to be happy, she
believed, whereas he was complacent to be wise.

Ballater, had she but known it, was far from complacent. Craddock had told him that he'd seen Rose visiting
Marshall at his cottage. To Craddock, Rose was an unex-
ploded bomb ticking away in Ballater's green and quiet
pasture at a time when the colonel should be enjoying
well-earned peace. It was unfair that circumstances
should have placed it there, and until it was defused (unlikely: her nature was unlikely to change) or removed
when she eventually took herself off, he watched it carefully. Had the musician not been married, he wouldn't
have reported back to his boss. But he was and there
might be trouble. Ballater had had trouble enough.

Rose was grooming the Charolais bull when Ballater
decided some plain speaking was necessary. The animal
was tethered in the byre, its hugely muscled body down
on its knees like a sacred beast from Indian mythology—
garlands around its horns would complete the picture.
She was brushing its neck with a long-handled brush
soaked in soapy water. He thought the picture not only
dangerous but grotesque, and was angry.

"That's a job for the men—I've warned you—get out
from there. Come out here."

She was wearing pale green dungarees, soaked with
muddy water, and looked like an untidy acolyte performing priestly duties in the priest's absence.

She put the brush back in the bucket. "He's safe. I've
reared him. He knows me."

"Do as I say!"

She sighed. There might be farming in her grandfather's blood, but the army was there more strongly still.
He treated her like an incompetent subaltern. She stepped
outside and secured the door. "Then who's to finish the
job? He can't be left like that."

"Craddock will see to it."

"Craddock and a couple of others." She was contemptuous.

Ballater saw one of the farm-hands going over to the cow-house and told him to fetch Craddock and see to the bull.

"And wear a suit of armour and carry a gun," Rose called out sarcastically. "He might hurt you."

His granddaughter's anger, so like his own, took some of the sting out of Ballater's wrath. He wished the quality of his care expressed his love for her more obviously—less abrasively. But he didn't know how to reach her. And didn't expect that he ever would.

"You're eighteen on the twentieth," he said, "the day after tomorrow."

"And so? I can't help it."

"I'm not accusing you of getting older. I'm just stating a fact. You're old enough to behave with some circumspection."

"In what way?"

"I hear you're seeing a lot of Marshall."

Craddock, she thought. What did he do—lie in the undergrowth and watch?

She explained about the kitten. "It's taking time to settle. Sometimes I stay and chat—not for long. I can't see any harm in that."

Put that way, it sounded reasonable. But he wasn't reassured. "I think you should be careful—for your sake and for his. I don't know why he's living in the cottage when he has a home elsewhere—and a wife."

"Nor do I," she said crisply, "but that's his business. His wife is called Zoe—and she's Lowell's affair—not yours—not mine."

He noticed the use of Christian names. The chats, then, had been personal. His anxiety grew. "It would be easy for her to become your affair, and that could be tragic for all of you."

"You have an odd idea of tragedy," she riposted. "What about the starving hordes in this wonderful world of ours? What about the bloody bomb?"

He refused to be side-tracked. "Has he made advances to you?"

By God, she thought, how old-fashioned could he be! "No," she said.

"You just go there and talk—what about?"

"He's writing a nocturne. We discuss music."

He tried to believe it. It was plausible. Perhaps he was looking for danger where none existed, though his instinct told him he wasn't. She needed the companionship of suitable young people, he thought, and here on the farm she wasn't getting it. The previous year she had amused herself with Greg Farrel, one of the agricultural students who had come to help with the harvest. He had lodged with Craddock and his wife in the village. Craddock in a year or two would be retiring and he would need a replacement. Later still, if his own health began to fail, the farm would have to be run by a competent manager. There was scope here for a young lad with ability. Someone who could be trained. It was a depressing prospect that the farm would one day be run by a stranger.

"There are times," he said bleakly, "when I wish your father had sired a son. Someone with farming enthusiasm and a lot of common sense. Life would be easier for all of us."

Rose, smiling wryly, apologised for her sex. He cut across her. "I've something for you. You might as well have it now." He took three twenty-pound notes out of his wallet. "Add that to your allowance and get yourself a birthday present. Take the car into Cheltenham tomorrow and buy a dress—your clothes are appalling."

She thanked him. That he should tarnish the gift with a criticism was in character.

Ballater waited awkwardly for the perfunctory thank-you kiss, giving her a few moments before turning away. It now seemed that Rose couldn't even bear to touch him.

EIGHT

"I have to call at the bank," Lowell told her, "so we'll do your birthday shopping in Bristol and we'll use the van." Rose had suggested Cheltenham and the Mercedes. The duo sounded very up-market, distinctly more so than Broadmead and the van. The farm obviously prospered.

His bank balance, he guessed, was being slowly eroded. He needed a statement of his account. He wished he didn't. It would give him great pleasure to write a large cheque for something special for Rose's birthday—a particularly splendid piece of jewellery, perhaps—but he couldn't. She wasn't a child any longer, or she wouldn't be after tomorrow. His lovely, timeless Rose had come of age.

It occurred to him as they drove that a particularly splendid piece of jewellery wouldn't suit her anyway. Today she wore a navy anorak (the morning had begun cloudy) and plum-coloured cords. He had persuaded her to wear her hair tied back from her face. As she had worn it before—long ago. He was careful not to make the connection too often in his mind—the idea was bizarre, better not to believe it, certainly it mustn't be spoken of—but at moments such as now he couldn't push it away—and didn't want to. Rose had died. Rose was alive again. Why not? Mystical nonsense? Many of the world's major

religions believed in reincarnation—the ongoing spirit—
and belief was a gut feeling. It couldn't be intellectual-
ised. The faithful went on believing despite all rational
argument. The Hindus, for instance—

She broke into his thoughts. "Did you remember to
feed the cat?"

"What?" The van gave an erratic burst of speed as his
foot prodded the accelerator. He slowed down. "Sorry.
What did you say—the cat? Yes, I did." Hauled back to
reality, he wondered if he had. He'd meant to. He'd kept
back a portion of corned beef for the purpose.

"Good," she said.

She was glad he liked Middy despite his being a bloody
nuisance at times. Male cats usually were. It had a habit
of jumping on the bed when they were making love and
clawing him. All the love scratches should be hers, he
once told her ruefully. Another man would have kicked it
to hell. Lowell was gentle.

There had been power in his music, she discovered. He
had played his cassettes to her and she had begun to understand what he had lost. His nocturne—*her* nocturne—
had started out like ice over dark water, he told her, and
then the ice had cleared and there was warmth in the
water, living things, beauty. He hoped some day someone
would play it—if it was worth playing.

She never knew how to respond to that sort of talk so
stayed silent. He made demands on her mentally and
emotionally. She had the odd feeling, at times, that she
was being moulded like a lump of clay into the person he
wanted her to be. His will was at times stronger than hers
—and that was something new. He wasn't a dominant
male chauvinist, he was tender and thoughtful—but he
was something more, and what that something was she
didn't understand. Which one of the reasons she
kept coming back.

Even though at times he scared her.

But that was part of the excitement of being loved. This was an Adult Experience. Capital *A*—Capital *E*. Wasn't it?

Parking in Bristol was difficult, as usual, but Lowell managed to find a slot in a multi-storey car park near Broadmead, the city's main shopping centre. She said she would shop for a couple of hours on her own, that she didn't want him with her while she mooched around dress departments. Unlike Zoe, she disliked buying clothes. They arranged to meet for lunch at a restaurant in Union Street.

He watched her making her way through the crowds on the pavement outside Lewis's, already looking bored at the prospect of spending her grandfather's money.

He wondered how much of his own he had left.

Half an hour later he knew.

Of the approximately one and a half thousand pounds from the sale of the Volvo, minus expenses, that he regarded legitimately as his, added to the four thousand in his and Zoe's joint account, there remained one hundred and seventy pounds. He couldn't get an immediate breakdown of where the money had gone, so asked to see the manager. The manager was unavailable, the clerk told him, would the chief accountant do? Anyone would do so long as he was able to explain how that much money could be spirited away in under four months.

The talk with the chief accountant in his plush office wasn't at first revealing. It was extremely easy in these days of high prices to spend that much money, he was told. Hire-purchase contracts. Mortgage. Heating bills—etc., etc. Lowell explained that they had no hire-purchase commitments and that the house was theirs. He had paid off the mortgage with ease when at the height of his success. As for heating bills—this was summer-time—what was his wife burning on the occasional days when it was cool—gold-dust? The accountant, realising he wouldn't be fobbed off, tried harder and came up with some facts. Mrs. Marshall had opened her own personal account. She was feeding it, but not drawing on it. Did that help to clarify the situation? It did. Zoe was bleeding the joint account dry. Lowell felt like a soldier on a battlefield, stripped of ammunition. This was Zoe's way of declaring war. He couldn't blame her. He was a selfish slob. An unrepentant selfish slob. He had no intention of changing his way of life, but how it was to be sustained now he had no idea.

He could, of course, join a few million others and draw the dole. Eventually it might come to that. It would mean a visit to his house to get his National Insurance card, and then going through the intricacies and humiliations of getting money from the State. Money he was entitled to, he reminded himself. But he wasn't ready yet to go back to his home and rummage around for documents. He wanted neither sight nor smell of the place. In time he would have to, but not yet. He was afraid of how he might react if he confronted Zoe now. It was safer not to see her.

He wrote himself a cheque for one hundred and sixty pounds, which left ten in the account, and took the money in tens rather than twenties; it looked bulkier, more reassuring. There was still over an hour to go before his rendezvous with Rose and he decided to walk around the jewellers' shops to find something he could afford.

Rose too, in her quest for a dress, became money-conscious. The stuff was either rubbish, or twee, or so boring it made you want to puke. If you wanted style you paid hundreds for it—so blow the sixty quid on something else—but what? She was wandering down an arcade when she saw the new Tissot boutique. There was a pair of dark maroon button boots in the window next to a lace fan and a parasol. They were grouped around a white metal table piled with gewgaws: hair ornaments, earrings, a necklace. The necklace, a small card stated, was made of butterfly wings. If that were true, and she couldn't believe it, how many butterflies had been killed, and how had the wings been put into the glass balls? Curious, she wandered into the shop. Once inside, she forgot the necklace. This, she discovered, was her sort of place.

It smelt of camphor as if the old clothes hanging on racks had just been taken out of ancient chests. It was a good smell. And the clothes felt good as she trailed her hand along them—thin cottons—muslins—fine wools—nothing synthetic. A large poster, spotlighted at the back of the shop, advertised the James Tissot exhibition currently showing at the art gallery. She had never heard of him but liked the picture of the Victorian women on board the HMS *Calcutta.* One wore a white dress with a yellow bow on her bottom. Rose chuckled. How would her grandfather respond to *that?*

A saleswoman came out from behind the counter and asked if she could help. "Just explain," Rose said, "who's Tissot—what's this place—what's it all about?"

Tissot, the saleswoman told her, was a French artist of the mid-nineteenth century, a contemporary of Degas. He specialised in portraits of the ladies of the period and was particularly interested in their clothing. His mistress modelled a lot of them. Her name was Mrs. Newton. "The exhibition," she went on, "will probably revive interest in the period, so we grabbed some of the stuff from our theatrical costumes shop up in Clifton and added it to the mixture of periods we have here. All copies, of course. The real stuff would cost a mint. What period are you interested in?"

"No period, just looking."

"If your mother was into flower-power in the sixties, these are the kind of clothes she would have worn." The saleswoman went over to a rack of ankle-length cottons in different colours.

"Flowers never powered my mother," Rose said drily.
But she was interested. One of the gowns made of dimity
appealed to her; the dark blue rib was decorated with
small green leaves. She asked if she might try it on—and
several more. They weren't her sort of clothes, she kept
telling herself. What good was an ankle-length dress on a
farm? And she wasn't the type of person to have frills
around her neck, for God's sake! Anything and everything was worn these days, the saleswoman urged. Knee
length—ankle length—all were in fashion. All it took was
self-confidence. And what was style, after all, but the
courage to be yourself? The clothes, she assured her,
would look right on her.

It was sales talk, but it was true.

Eventually she bought a maroon dress with a crocheted
collar and a matching bolero which hid a small repaired
split under the arm. Superb quality and a good choice, the
saleswoman enthused. As it had been hired out for stage
work a few times and wasn't perfect, the selling price was
thirty-five pounds.

Which left cash enough for a second-hand cloak of
black wool and the button boots in the window—if they
fitted. They did.

Rose, never interested in clothes before, tried the lot on
and beamed at herself in the long mirror. She looked *fantastic.* Her grandfather would be furious.

Laden with parcels, she was half an hour late for her
luncheon appointment, and Lowell, seated at a table near
the window, was already waiting for her. Drinking his
beer as if it had gone flat, she thought, seeing him before
he saw her. What was the matter? She was happy. She
didn't want gloom.

"All my clothes are second-hand," she told him by way
of greeting. "I love them. You'll hate them. What have
you been doing with yourself?"

Resisting making myself bankrupt, he nearly said, by

not buying a gold locket I coveted for you—delicate—beautiful—too bloody expensive.

He told her he'd drawn some money from the bank. Not a lot. And bought her a birthday present. That was second-hand, too. And she wouldn't like it.

"Try me." She pushed her parcels under the table and held out her hand.

"It isn't your birthday until tomorrow."

"I can't wait."

"You can for this." He was depressed—suddenly ashamed of the gift.

Sensing it, she changed the subject and told him about the Tissot exhibition. "Let's go and see it after we've eaten. I don't want much—a pizza or something will do."

"Damn it, I can afford to give you a decent meal."

"I'm not hungry now. For God's sake—why argue about food?" She picked up the menu. "If you don't want to go to the exhibition—say so."

"I've no objection to going—if that's what you want to do."

"I do—unless you have a better idea?"

He hadn't.

Lowell parked the van just off Queen's Road, within a couple of minutes' walk of the City Museum and Art Gallery. The exhibition was set up in a room housing the work of early nineteenth-century local artists, including Francis Danby. The Frenchman's style was an interesting comparison. For Lowell, twentieth-century Rose was an even more interesting comparison. He followed a little behind her, intrigued by her reaction to the various scenes. *The Social Climber* amused her. "Just look at that man's lecherous eyes." She was bored by the girl in *The Bunch of Lilacs,* but the portrait of Kathleen Newton appealed. "What do you suppose that book is under her arm—the *Decameron?* She was his mistress, you know."

Lowell didn't. "Where did you pick up that piece of salacious gossip?"

"In a shop—earlier today."

"This conversation is unbelievable. Elucidate."

He was smiling. She was glad he was happy again.

A concert in the Victoria Rooms, a little further up the road, was the next natural sequence in a day that seemed planned. The evening performance—a Mozart symphony —didn't start until seven and it would mean a late return home. She would have to phone her grandfather and tell him, she said, and she had to get into the van for her purse. Lowell told her that he would finance the phone call, he had plenty of small change. She declined. There was something else she needed from the van. So he gave her the keys.

He went ahead of her to the concert hall, bought the tickets, and stood waiting for her in the foyer. Coming here—even with Rose—wasn't easy. On his own—or with Zoe—it would have been impossible. He had performed here many times in the past, and the passive role was hard to take. He wanted to make music—an angry torrent of sound—and was jealous to the gut of the young soloist who was going to perform at *his* piano on *his* stage tonight.

Edwin Leeson echoed his thoughts, startling him. "Hello, Lowell—at the wrong end of things, aren't you? How are you?"

The photographer and his wife Jane had been about to go through into the concert hall when Leeson saw Lowell standing on his own.

Lowell said his hands were protesting.

"They're no better?"

"Never better enough."

Jane strolled over. "Long time no see, Lowell." He agreed it had been. Not seeing Jane, however, was no

cause for regret; she had none of the kindly qualities of
her husband. Physically she resembled a smoothly
groomed Pekinese with large lambent eyes, a silken-
haired little bitch. Her curiosity now was obvious. He
hoped she wouldn't voice it. She did, but in a roundabout
way. "Zoe's not joining the crafts class this autumn, nor
the keep-fit. It's bad enough for one member of the family to hibernate—can't you persuade her?"

He didn't answer.

She coloured a little. Had he ditched his wife, or had
she ditched him? His silence was chilling, but she pressed
on. "I met her in town one day last week. I didn't think
she looked well. Pale with shock, perhaps; she'd just
bought herself a mink."

This time Leeson broke the silence before it froze over
too hard. "I'm here on a photographic assignment; the
camera is temporarily parked in the ticket office. Do you
know young Bennet, the soloist?"

Lowell's brain was ticking over figures like a demented
computer—so that was where the money was going—a
mink jacket, or a mink coat—whichever, it was goodbye
to a thousand plus. He stopped thinking about his hands.

Leeson repeated the question.

"Yes," Lowell said, "or rather—no. I know of Bennet. I
haven't heard him play."

"Then you've a treat in store. He has all the talent you
had at his age. He's playing one of your favourites, too—
the C Minor."

"Good." She would have bought accessories to go with
it. Handbag. Shoes.

"He would be proud to know you were sitting in the
audience tonight." Leeson's comment was honest. It
wasn't empty flattery.

"I doubt it." And jewellery, possibly. Something even
more expensive than the gold locket.

"Well, very much on his mettle, certainly. You're hard

to follow." And damned hard to converse with—what the hell's wrong with you?

Leeson was looking around for inspiration, a topic of conversation that didn't rub salt into wounds, but what he saw silenced him with shock. The girl of the urn, he thought. It couldn't be, but it was.

Lowell had seen her too. His heartbeat quickened as Rose approached. At last the confirmation of something he had known for a long time. He was stunned into silence as longing and relief surged through him.

Rose had changed into the Victorian clothes in the van. And tidied her hair. She wore no make-up. She never did. Lowell looked at her with deep loving awareness. "Yes," she said, "it's me." She touched his hand with unusual gentleness. "If you have the tickets," she said, "I suggest we go in."

It was halfway through a brilliant performance that Lowell scarcely heard when he remembered the present he'd bought her. The second-hand necklace he'd thought was wrong was suddenly right. It was delicate pink coral and enhanced her maroon dress better than gold. She leaned over to him as he fastened it around her throat.

A few seats behind them Jane Leeson nudged her husband. "Oh my, oh my," she whispered, "just wait till I tell Zoe!"

Leeson didn't respond. He'd had a sudden sick recollection of the headline in the *Illustrated Police News,* dated 1870, which he had found in the library archives. The atmosphere was rank with menace. Needing air, he got up abruptly—wishing to Christ that Lowell would take his thick ugly fingers off the girl's neck.

NINE

"If it were Ben," Louise told Zoe, "I wouldn't wage a long slow war of attrition, or whatever it is you're doing, I'd go to the cottage and raise hell."

She watched Zoe's stooped figure as she cleared away some dead summer bedding. It was a wonder she hadn't paid the part-time gardener extra cash to do it for her; perhaps the money in the joint account had run out. Zoe had admitted her tactics in a weak moment, but sensing Louise's disgust hadn't referred to them since.

"But it's not Ben"—Zoe stood up and held her back, which was beginning to ache—"and that's the difference."

"You're not still afraid of him?"

Zoe dodged the question. "I see things differently, that's all." She picked up the trowel and a bag of tulip bulbs. "I'll plant these later. Come in for coffee?"

"Better have it in my place, I have to watch the kids."

A heart-to-heart in a domestic atmosphere which smelt of burnt rice pudding tended to lose some of its pain. Clarissa was asleep in her carry-cot and Christopher was painting noisily at his easel.

Zoe tried to explain, keeping her voice low on account of the boy: she'd thought Lowell was in love with a Victorian photograph—and that was crazy. She saw now that it was probably a photograph of the bitch he was going to bed with. Jane Leeson had mentioned a girl in fancy dress. So he wasn't sick in his head—just unfaithful —and that was a mild way of putting it. She'd put it differently but certain little people might be listening.

Louise looked at her young son and suggested he might like to take his easel onto the patio. It was cold out there, he protested, and why was Zoe whispering? Didn't she know it was rude?

Ten minutes later, installed in the comparative quietness of the sitting-room, Louise did some gentle probing. Had Jane described her—not just the dress—the way she looked?

Zoe wasn't keen to talk about it any more. That child had been impertinent. Louise should bring him up better. If she and Lowell had had a child . . . she wouldn't let the thought form.

She shrugged. "Long hair worn in a chignon. She had to lift up a few loose strands from her neck when Lowell fastened the beads."

"Beads?"

"That's what she called them."

The girl with the cat had long hair, too, Louise remembered, but it was worn loose. It could be the same one. The memorable part of the meeting had been Lowell's eagerness to be with her.

"Did Jane tell you anything else?"

It wasn't what Jane had told her that had carried the conversation along as much as what Jane had implied. Lowell had seemed interested, she'd said. And her lips had closed firmly while her eyes had told Zoe the rest. The bitch had knocked him cold. Message received and understood?

"She thought there was probably a *friendship*." Zoe smiled bitterly. "Lowell had walked off with her without introducing them. I've told you all this before."

"It doesn't necessarily add up to going to bed." But it probably did. Zoe's instinct could be right. "I still think you ought to go and have it out with him."

Zoe was silent.

Louise struggled not to say it—and lost. "Ben and I will go with you if you want us to." She had already suggested this to Ben, and he hadn't been co-operative. He'd gone the last time, he reminded her, because of Lowell's hands—well, partly. He belonged to the medical profession, not to the Sally Army. If Lowell had another woman, that was his business and Zoe's. The affair had a different dimension now. It wasn't just a case of depression and withdrawal any more. So don't interfere.

"I don't think there's any use going to see him," Zoe said. "Not yet."

She changed the subject. "Did he tell you how much the farmer had offered for the cottage?"

"No. Apparently he wants access to the lower road."

"Did Lowell mention his name?"

Louise had a good memory. "Yes, Ballater. He owns the farm over the hill." She took Zoe's mug and poured her fresh coffee. "But you can't do anything about that, can you? The cottage is in Lowell's name."

No, Zoe agreed, she couldn't do anything about that. But time would, she thought. And the more presents he gave his whore, the shorter that time would be. She wondered if she should hire a private detective to find out who the girl was. But did it matter who she was? Giving her a name didn't help the situation. In a way it made it worse.

She took a sip of coffee from the thick earthenware mug. Her last large expenditure had been on a Royal Doulton tea-service. Very beautiful. Had she been wise she would have bought the matching coffee cups. It would have hastened the end.

Oh dear God, why did she want to laugh and cry at the
same time? Why was Louise looking at her like that?

"I think it would be a good thing," she said stiffly, not
meaning it, "if Lowell and I had a divorce."

Louise was silent.

"He's on my back like an old man of the sea."

And you want him there, Louise thought, you really
do. Zoe—uptight—prim—was throbbing away with hurt,
anger, loneliness. Was it possible to feel that way without
love? Or was it self-love? Anyway, who was she to
judge? There were many ways of fighting for your man—
most of them nasty.

Rose came to him by night now.

Though he wasn't to know this, it was a gesture of
defiance, that was slowly becoming a sexual need. Her
grandfather's anger at her late return from Bristol—especially as she had gone there with Marshall—had been
explosive. He had expected her back by midnight at the
latest, judging by the phone call and the length of the
concert, so where had she been until two in the morning?
She told him that Cinderella's coach had broken down—a
puncture. They had, in fact, arrived at Lowell's cottage
well before midnight and made love. The September
moon had sent its beams over the bed and into the corners of the bedroom so that everything seemed vivid,
rather stark, a little ghostly. He had walked her home
afterwards, though she had wanted to stay. She had refused to let him go right up to the house. If there was
aggro she could handle it. She was, after all, eighteen.
Officially adult. Her life was her own to live as she
wished.

Lowell's conscience ebbed and flowed when he thought
of Ballater and the old man's anxiety. Rose stemmed the
flow, encouraged the ebb, and he allowed it to be that
way. What harm was there in this strange, delightful,

mind-bending relationship? He had never felt so fulfilled, so much at peace with himself. Life had started dealing him aces again; the joker with the twisted hands was now relegated to the bottom of the pack.

It began to resurface when Greg Farrel walked into the cottage with the swaggering confidence of a man who had walked into it many times before. It was seven o'clock in the evening and Lowell was mashing up cat biscuits in hot water for Middy.

Both men were equally startled.

Lowell saw a tall young redhead of about twenty-two dressed in motorcycle gear. Before he spoke Lowell knew he'd be brash and loud-mouthed, a son of a bitch.

Farrel sensed the antagonism. "Oh!" he exclaimed. "Who are you?"

"I was about to ask you the same question." The kitten was clawing at Lowell's trouser leg and he put the food down on the floor. It was extremely hot. Middy, about to lick it delicately, took a leap backwards.

Farrel watched with interest. Feeding a resident animal implied that the bloke with the food was resident, too.

"The door was open," he explained, by way of an apology. "I thought Rose was here."

"It would help to advance our understanding of each other," Lowell retorted coldly, "if you told me who you are."

Farrel mimicked Lowell's pedantic voice inside his head, but he hadn't the guts to initiate a confrontation. "Greg Farrel," he said, and extended his hand. "How do you do, sir?" The older generation, he had discovered, liked the courtesy title.

Lowell ignored the hand. "You still haven't told me why you've walked into my property—and what have you to do with Rose?"

His property? Farrel had always thought this was Bal-

later's place. A farm cottage that Rose had commandeered
for her own use from time to time.

"So Ballater sold it to you?" he said. "I see." He added,
"I think the kitten has burnt its tongue." Middy was lick-
ing its chest furiously.

Lowell explained that he'd inherited the cottage from a
member of his family. "Why did you expect to find Rose
here?" He was alarmed at the possibility that this lad was
from the village and that the village was rife with gossip.

Farrel explained that he was an agricultural student and
had come to lend a hand with the harvest. "I was here last
year. It's a holiday job. Rose liked to come down here
when the old man got on her wick."

He wondered if the new owner were a confidant of
Ballater. Possible. So tell him nothing more.

Lowell felt a niggling sense of betrayal. Rose had admitted coming here when Miss Marshall was alive. Why
hide from him the fact that she had been coming since?
Was this the yob who had planted the cannabis? He suddenly remembered her carefully veiled amusement when
he had mentioned the tinkers. Things began fitting damn-
ingly into place.

Farrel decided it would be wise to lay new tracks
through the forest—for Rose's sake. He had blundered in
here, and it would be necessary to withdraw by another
route. "Colonel Ballater is a competent farmer," he said,
"considering he came to it late. And he can't think too
badly of me or he wouldn't have invited me back this
year. I'm staying at the farmhouse—last year I lodged in
the village." He bent down and patted Middy. "Nice
moggie. Rose has a gift with animals. Have you seen her
handling that whacking great bull?" He babbled on without waiting for an answer. "Most of the other agricultural
students have to take holiday jobs away from farming—

some of them prefer to. I don't. It'll be good to help get the harvest in—sweaty hard work—satisfying."

Lowell sensed he was being diverted. The honest farm-lad building stoops of corn—or the modern equivalent. It was a comforting diversion; he told himself not to question it too deeply and accept it for now. Politeness, at this stage, demanded an introduction. It was his turn to hold out his hand. "I'm Lowell Marshall, nothing to do with farming at all."

But the name meant nothing to the visitor; obviously his fame hadn't penetrated the student community. But when Farrel shook his hand he saw Lowell wince and realised he'd gripped too hard. The bloke was arthritic. "Sorry," he apologised, "damned hard luck, sir." It was the tone he adopted with Colonel Ballater—very Colonel Blimpish. Not the right tone for this man, he sensed. He hadn't his measure yet. Why, for example, was he so interested in Rose?

"What is it you do, then, Mr. Marshall?"

The obsession of the doers, Lowell thought, was always to push the non-doers into categories. Marshall the ex-musician. At the present time, he told Farrel, he wasn't doing anything. His expression warned him to leave it at that.

An academic on a sabbatical, Farrel wondered? Rose would know. "It wouldn't be your van down by the bottom field, would it?" He clearly expected a reply in the negative.

Lowell said it was. "At a guess, more comfortable than your motorbike. You came on one, I think?"

Farrel said he had. "It's parked down by your van. There's still no road access to the farm from here."

"No." Not while I hold on to my cottage, there isn't.

"Then I'll have to drive over to Ballater's on the other road."

Which you would have done in the first place, Lowell thought, if you hadn't been so sure that Rose was here.

This lad and Rose were of an age.

Some of the light was leaving the day.

TEN

It took Greg Farrel a few days to realise he was being vetted, both socially and professionally. It was an uncomfortable experience. Ballater ran the farm like a military exercise. He was a good strategist, delegated carefully, and made full use of computers, working from his office most of the time. Living in the house, Farrel soon discovered, was like being a very junior NCO in a senior officers' mess. Evening meals, he guessed, would be hell. Last year he had thought Rose was exaggerating when she described the experience. "You scrape around in your head for something to talk about," she'd said, "and you sip wine from Waterford crystal. Your feet get hot in your bloody shoes and you want to go outside and walk through mud."

That just about summed it up. There were limits to what one could say about milk yields and the EEC. The views of the tutors at the agricultural college weren't necessarily the same as the stern-looking old man's, and he didn't know enough about anything yet to enter into an argument. Anyway, an argument was bad policy. It was good policy to listen politely and say yes. It was good policy to apologise, charmingly if possible, for not having brought more suitable clothes. Jazzy T-shirts and jeans were all he had.

He wondered how much the farm was worth.

Rose, watching him across the shining mahogany table, guessed what he was wondering.

That first evening they went walking up the hill away from Marshall's cottage, to a small plantation of aspen trees. There was a grassy hollow nearby, not a totally private place but well out of sight of the farm. Here the chuntering sound of a tractor could be heard in the distance, and the gentle lowing of beasts. Close at hand was the skittering of a small animal through the grass and the dry fragile sound of leaves turning.

Rose said, "I'm still me. I hate it when my grandfather tries to plan my life."

He understood her.

Even so, the plan might not be a bad one. Archaic, of course, but it had its points. His family couldn't afford to set him up as an independent farmer. His father, annoyed that he hadn't followed family tradition and become a solicitor, had made the hoary old joke about marrying a rich man's daughter.

In this case—granddaughter.

And desirable.

He moved his hand gently over Rose's breasts.

She made it even plainer. "I hate farming. One day I'll leave here. I'll never stay."

Perhaps so, but she might be persuaded.

She moved his hand aside impatiently. Compared with Lowell he was an amateur: clumsy and insensitive. "Did you bring any pot?" she asked.

He had, but in these new circumstances it might be unwise to admit it. "No."

The hesitation before he replied had been a fraction too long. She grinned at him. "Did you know that *kif* is Moroccan for peace and tranquillity? I could do with both—so give."

It wasn't on him. It was in his luggage. He might admit

to having it later on, but he wasn't sure yet what he was going to do; it would be stupid to queer the pitch at this early stage of the game.

If you were protecting me for my own good, she thought, I would be cross with you, but not this cross. "For God's sake," she snapped, "the stuff's harmless!"

"Maybe—but it's not legal—and you got into trouble before."

"If you're going to start trotting out the right answers for the wrong reasons you'll go down great with my grandfather. What are you doing now—practising?"

She was beginning to annoy him. And excite him. There was something different about her this year. She was, to a degree, indifferent to him—and even to the cannabis. He guessed she didn't care all that much whether he handed it over or not. So where was she getting her kicks?

It was only after several days of hard work harvesting, rounded off by celibate nights, that he discovered why Rose kept her bedroom door locked.

She locked it because she wasn't in it.

It was by chance that he saw her, close to midnight, making her way towards the bottom road. At first he thought she might be sleep-walking. Her long dress looked like an old fashioned night-gown. But Rose wouldn't wear anything in bed. And she walked as if she knew where she was going. By the time he left his bedroom and took the path across the field she was out of sight. He walked a little way along the road, past Marshall's van, and couldn't find her. The only place she could disappear into in that space of time was Marshall's cottage. He retraced his footsteps and stayed around for a while, but it was too cold to linger long. The next night he wore his leather jacket and warm boots and positioned himself near the field where the Charolais cattle grazed— the vantage point that Rose had used to watch Lowell's

cottage before she knew him. She returned just after
dawn.

In the early morning light he could see that she wore a
black cape over a dark red dress. He hadn't seen either
before. Her hair was messed up as if she'd come straight
from bed, and her cheeks despite the coolness of the day
were flushed as if she'd recently made love.

She hadn't seen him, but she sensed someone might be
there and glanced over her shoulder. He moved backwards into the lee of the wall. She shrugged and walked
on quietly to the house. The front door was ajar. She
knew now who it was and stood waiting in the hall until
Greg joined her.

Abashed at being caught spying, his tone was aggressive: "Had a good time?"

"The best ever." Her eyes were mocking.

"Does the old man know?"

"Don't be ridiculous." She wondered what price his
silence might be.

But he had no price. He liked her. His pride was hurt.
His body was young, strong; last year she had delighted
in it. Had her new lover been one of his pals it would be
insulting—but not this insulting.

He said the first thing that came into his head. "He's
weird. The cottage is macabre. And your dress looks like
a bloody red shroud."

She made a V-sign turned the wrong way—a silent ex-
pletive—and made for the stairs.

That evening at dinner Greg asked Ballater about Marshall's cottage. "I always thought the place belonged to
you, sir."

Ballater said he hoped that one day it would. He sensed
that the conversation must have a point, but he wasn't
sure what it was. Greg said he'd met Marshall briefly.
"He says he has no farming connections."

Ballater explained Marshall's background while Rose listened silently.

"Does he ever come up to visit you, sir?"

Ballater answered smoothly that he hadn't invited him. "Remiss of me, but I tend not to socialise." He added drily, "Rose attended a concert with him."

"Classical music," Rose broke in. "Not really your kind of thing, Greg." It was safer to guide the conversation in another direction. "He happened to be going to Bristol and drove me in. I went shopping for clothes."

"And didn't get any," her grandfather observed, "or if you did, I haven't seen them."

"There wasn't anything suitable." The clothes were for Lowell. For the cottage. For the person she became when she went there. Greg's jibe about the dress being like a shroud rankled. He'd been talking shit.

"I like rock music; something with a good thumping beat to it." Greg mimed it with his fingers on the edge of the table and looked at Rose. "You like it, too."

She understood the sexual implications of the mime and hoped her grandfather didn't.

But her fears were groundless: the generation gap in this instance had him beached on a far shore. The boy had stated a preference, that was all. Rock music went on in discotheques, he supposed. They were places of revolving lights and gyrating bodies. Natural meeting places for today's moronic young.

He told Farrel he had no objection if he wanted to take Rose to a discotheque, provided they returned at a reasonable hour. "Use the small car," he suggested. "The Peugeot."

When it had gone midnight Lowell knew she wasn't coming. The cat, sitting on his knee, yawned and stretched voluptuously. One of its paws gently brushed

Lowell's neck, a feather-light touch, the claws neatly en-
cased in fur. Ash from the log whispered in the fireplace.

The room was lit by candles, as Rose disliked the smell
of his paraffin lamp. He focused his attention on them,
concentrating on trivia, blocking out anxiety. He remembered the tall thin red ones Zoe used to put in the silver
candelabra when she was entertaining. Candles for effect.
It was difficult to read by candle-light. Or to compose. So
he worked on the nocturne by day, mindful of the con-
tradiction.

He tended to talk a lot inside his head when Rose
wasn't there. A dialogue with himself. Controllable. He
told himself she wasn't coming—that there was a perfectly good reason for her absence. She wasn't lying dead
in a field—mugged—raped. She had always insisted that
he wasn't to meet her, that she might come any time. Or
not come at all.

The dialogue tonight might be controlled and rational
—but it gave him no ease. He couldn't just sit here and do
nothing.

He put Middy down, found the torch, and went walking up the field path. The cat prowled after him, padding
softly through the dark grass. The night air had a rank
sweaty smell like the distilled essence of anxiety. There
was no sweetness anywhere. His torch made yellow arcs
across the hedgerows. Snaked through the undergrowth.
Probed. Searched and found nothing. The sky, dizzy with
stars, made him vertiginous and he stumbled and fell.
Everything was too vast—too silent—too dark. He sat
crouching where he had fallen, his head resting on his
knees, his hands over his eyes. Not moving. Disorientated. Time seemed to have stopped. He was aware of
nothing other than the necessity to breathe.

Middy rubbed softly against him, and the trance—almost cataleptic—was broken. Bemused, a little fright-
ened, he got slowly to his feet and looked around him. He

was here in familiar fields. Everything was normal. There was nothing wrong. Just an odd reaction. A queer mood. It had passed.

He walked up the hill near the farm and then, reaching the summit, gazed down at the farmhouse. A few pale lights shone at the windows, but there was no sign of Rose. Of anyone.

After a while he persuaded himself to turn back. To look for her was an intrusion of her privacy. She might be with that redheaded yob. If he came on them in the darkness and they were . . . but she wouldn't . . . it was perfectly natural . . . she was eighteen and he . . . He forced himself to say it and spoke aloud: "They might be making love. Go back to your own bed. Accept it."

When he returned to the cottage he extinguished all but one of the candles and took it through to the bedroom. The bed looked cold, uninviting. For Christ's sake, he *couldn't* accept it! He wanted her. Needed her. If she went from him permanently, he didn't know what he'd do.

There were times when Rose felt as if she were split in half—an interesting rather than a painful experience. Two men wanted her. Two men had her—in different degrees. Sex with Greg was improving a little; he was learning to be less selfish, to think of her pleasure. It was an easy, calm relationship—no hassle—no tension—no acting.

When she was with Lowell she was on a pedestal—she couldn't even swear—but his love-making was fantastic. Together in the cottage, in bed, she felt like exploding with love for him. Out of bed he was less perfect. How could a man so intelligent in every other way be so obtuse when it came to ordinary everyday living? She liked the cottage as much as he did, it cast its own peculiar spell, but it wasn't something out of Grimm. It didn't

have walls of gingerbread. The larder wasn't magic; it
didn't restock itself. And he was running out of fuel for
the fire. The van, he told her, was an unexpected expense.
He had to have a new battery for it, and two of the tyres
weren't legal. Put simply, the thrill of flaunting Grandfather's wishes was beginning to pall.

While Greg was living up at the farm she forgot to
bring down milk for the cat. When he went back to college she began to remember again. In the meantime Lowell had made do with powdered milk for both him and
the animal. He saw the omission as a symptom of a tem-
porary aberration. When the milk began coming again he
hoped the aberration was over. Rose had had fun with a
boy of her own age. He had gone. She would forget him.
It was the voice of reason. Forced. Necessary. Unconvinc-
ing.

Rose thought she would forget Greg, too, but it wasn't
so easy. He wrote letters to her, funny ones with a few
clumsy sentences about missing her. He wasn't in residence at the college now and had a small flat in Gloucester. If her grandfather removed the ball and chain, he
wrote, would she visit? She knew that he had an eye to
the future; the farm was a desirable property. He didn't
love her as Lowell loved her, but he probably loved her as
much as he was capable of loving anyone. His shallow
waters were becoming more comfortable to dabble in
than Lowell's dark and turbid sea. That it was becoming
darker, more turbid, as time went on disturbed her. He
seemed to want to possess her, body and soul. It was the
soul she jibbed at. She had her own thoughts and her
own way of expressing them. With Lowell a lot had to be
edited out before she spoke.

But she couldn't control her dreams and sometimes she
talked in her sleep. Lowell, holding her, made little sense
of what she was saying. It was something about a child.
Once she woke up crying.

He stroked her hair back from her forehead. "What is it? Tell me."

"I don't know. I can't remember." The dream was fractured into a kaleidoscope of shapes that refused to form into a coherent whole. There was a voice—accusatory, though unclear—a jumble of words inducing a strong feeling of guilt. Fully awake, she was able to block its message. But it remained, mocking her, at the centre of the nightmare.

She sat up in bed, freeing herself from Lowell's arms. "What time is it?"

He lit the bedside candle and looked at his watch. "Twenty past one."

Her maroon dress was flung over the back of a chair by the window. The boots, neatly placed side by side, were near the bed. It could be the stage setting of a period play, she thought, but it wasn't. It was an autumn night in the 1980s—and an autumn night a hundred or more years ago. The latter felt the more real. It was ghostly. Scary.

It was also inconvenient.

"Lowell, I need to go to the loo." The loo was bloody outside.

He got out of bed. "Wait until I get my torch. I'll come with you."

She was trying to shove her hot feet into her button boots. It was all so damned stupid, so damned bloody fucking ridiculous. "It's raining—I should have wellies."

She was crying again, this time with exasperation. He hugged her—his gorgeous, beautiful Rose.

She pushed him away. "Don't! I'm in a *hurry.*"

They went down the garden path, shielded by his big black umbrella. When they returned she didn't want to go back to bed. She wanted to go home. It was the first time she had left him before dawn.

· · · ·

The idyll was breaking. He couldn't—wouldn't—admit it. She was part of his life. Part of the cottage. Her destiny was here.

He tried to explain it to her, but she didn't know what he was talking about. He was wise enough not to be too explicit. He'd found a photograph of someone like her, he said. Some time in the past she had belonged to the cottage, as Rose belonged to it now.

Where was the photograph? she wanted to know.

His wife had destroyed it.

But why?

He shrugged. "It doesn't matter. I have you."

They were sitting in the firelight, the candles making little red tongues of flame in the dark corners of the room. She fancied they were repeating what he said: I have you . . . I have you . . . I have you . . .

She had filched a bottle of claret from her grandfather's stock and they had been drinking it liberally. Perhaps it was the wine speaking. Wine made you a little light-headed—but it also soothed. So why this persistent feeling of unease?

She had never looked more lovely, he thought, and told her so. The soft fall of her hair over her shoulders gleamed red in places. The dark pink of the coral necklace had trapped a tendril before curving downwards to the small swell of her breasts. He leaned over and disentangled it.

"You must never cut your hair."

She moved impatiently. She must never do this. She must never do that.

"If I were painting a portrait of you, I'd call it Rose by Firelight."

"Lowell, do you want to go to bed with me?" Her voice was crisp. "Because if you do, you'd better start undoing all these goddamned buttons while the fire's still hot."

He winced.

At the "goddamned," she wondered? Or at the way she'd said it? Both, probably: she'd rocked the pedestal.

Later, in bed, she was back in character again. He knew how to make her body come alive.

"I love you," she told him, as she'd told him many times before. Three easy words that expressed her physical joy. Words he wanted to hear. Words she tended to forget when she was up and away from him.

The relationship, Lowell realised, had reached the stage when it needed to move onwards more positively. Rose, despite their love-making, was becoming restless. Impatient. She deserved better than these clandestine meetings. He hadn't thought of marriage before. Now he did. It was daunting. A divorce from Zoe—if she could be persuaded. The selling up of the house. If he and Zoe had half each, it would give him about forty thousand pounds' worth of capital. If Zoe agreed. But why should she? The honourable thing would be to give her the house. She hadn't transgressed, he had. Odd word—transgressed. Fornication—even odder. He couldn't feel they related to anything he'd done.

But Rose might not want to marry him. If she didn't, what did she want? A tarting up of the cottage—an inside lavatory? A few expensive gifts? Holidays together? A firm step into the twentieth century and all the comfort that money could bring . . . if he had any.

He couldn't believe it. Zoe was the materialist—not Rose. Zoe set store by the unimportant. Rose had different values. Rose was a girl to write music for. To dream about. To please.

But how?

What was he to do to hold her to him? To stop the drift? What course of action should he take? He was like a traveller dithering at crossroads, unsure which way to go.

ELEVEN

Jane Leeson went into the photographic studio and told her husband that Lowell's girlfriend was in the reception area. "She thinks she can just waltz in and have her photograph taken now."

Most people did. Sometimes they were lucky.

Today Leeson had a free hour before attending a wedding. To slot in a portrait was possible. If he wanted to.

"You *do* have the time," Jane pointed out. But not the inclination, she sensed. Her husband's reaction to Lowell's bit on the side had been subdued. He hadn't wanted to talk about her. "Lowell isn't with her," she said. "He's had the decency to keep away. So, from that point of view, it's not embarrassing."

Embarrassment wasn't the inhibiting factor. Leeson was perturbed.

"You can't mix business with friendship," Jane urged, "and anyway the friendship isn't that close. There's no reason why you shouldn't take the photograph."

Leeson, by nature taciturn, had told her very little about the original photograph and nothing at all about the research he and the Bristol archivist had done on it. Apart from anything else, history wasn't really her thing.

"What is she wearing?"

"Just the usual clobber kids wear these days—a yellow

T-shirt—bib-and-brace denims. She has a canvas bag, so perhaps there's something more suitable in that. Shall I send her in?"

Rose, who hadn't any recollection of the Leesons, had been surprised by Jane Leeson's expression when she had walked into the shop. On reflection she believed it was something to do with the way she looked—her casual dress. The women in the portraits on the wall wore a sleek assortment of cashmere and pearls or simple expensive-looking dresses.

The photograph would, Rose believed, be a tactful way of hinting that she didn't intend being around so much. She and Greg had exchanged snaps when he left. No problem there. No soul-searching. But with Lowell nothing was easy. He was getting too intense. Too serious. It was time to cool it.

There was a dressing-room off the reception area, she noticed, and when the receptionist returned she offered to go and change. But she was told to go straight in; Leeson's time was precious.

Leeson had hoped that his imagination had exaggerated the resemblance, but he saw when the girl walked in that it hadn't. The woman in the Victorian photograph and this girl had ties of blood. There had to be a relationship. Though separated by several generations it showed strongly. He observed the tilt of her chin and the curve of her cheekbones as she took in her surroundings.

Rose turned her attention to him, feeling a little disconcerted by the keenness of his gaze. "Well," she smiled, after the preliminary introduction, "do I pass whatever test you have?"

"What do you mean?"

"I guess you pick and choose. Am I photogenic?"

She was. Very. Like her ancestor: an unlucky beauty.

He tried to find a compromise that would satisfy his artistic urge and quieten his conscience. There was a chair on a small platform in front of the screen. He told her to go and sit on it.

"You mean—just as I am?"

"Yes."

"To try and fix a pose—or something? I have to change before you take me."

Lowell took you, Leeson thought grimly, into his bed. It was macabre.

"I just want to look at you for a moment or two." Her clothes were as different as possible from the Victorian get-up of the other one. Her face was young and fresh and shouldn't be shadowed—but shadows would be necessary. She would have to do something about her hair.

"Have you ever thought of pulling your hair back— plaiting it?"

"Not since I was in school."

"I think it would suit you that way."

"Well, I don't. The way I wear my hair has to suit my dress." Rose left the chair and picked up the canvas bag. "It's in here." She took it out and held it in front of her, the deep rich red material glowing against her skin. "There's a coral necklace to go with it."

He commented brusquely that he'd seen her in it before—at the concert. "You were with Lowell Marshall."

She thought she was beginning to understand. These people were friends of Lowell—and perhaps of his wife. They didn't approve.

"That's right. I was with Lowell. The photograph is for him."

"Then you must let me take it my way."

"Your way? What do you mean?"

He talked a little about artistic interpretation without much hope of her agreeing. "You're young—fresh—very much of this day and age. I want to enhance that. The clothes you're wearing now are just right. I like the way you look, apart from your hair. It needs tying back."

"Lowell likes it arranged more formally, swept off my face, but not in a plait."

"It spoils the gamine look."

"But I'm not gamine. He doesn't see me that way. I have to pose in the Victorian dress and with my hair the way I told you." She ran her fingers through it in exasperation. "Not this untidy—I'll comb it."

"Please—it has to be my way."

She realised with astonishment that he was actually pleading. Then he added: "Or not at all."

"You mean—you want me to go somewhere else."

"No." He had to give some sort of explanation.

"If Lowell asked you to have your portrait taken in period dress, I think he was unwise. He wasn't seeing you clearly. I think he should appreciate you for what you are —an attractive young woman of today."

"But he sees me the other way—he spoke of another photograph—he was telling me that . . ."

He interrupted her. "Then you haven't seen it—the one Lowell had enlarged?"

"No. Why? What about it? Was it a nude or something?"

"No, not a nude. A Victorian woman posed by an urn."

She remembered the carved piece of stone that Lowell held in his hand sometimes—part of an urn, he'd told her.

"What's wrong with that? Why shouldn't I pose that way if it pleases him?"

He spoke unguardedly. "I think it's a bit sick."

"Sick? What do you mean?"

He regretted the indiscretion and didn't answer.

She was getting worried. "Why is it sick to dress like someone from the past? Who was she, anyway?"

"It doesn't matter—just someone who lived a long time ago—best forgotten."

"But—why? What happened to her?"

It was becoming increasingly difficult to prevaricate.

"I suppose these days she'd be called a victim of circumstances. She lived not far from where I think Lowell's cottage is—somewhere in that area. And then she moved to London with her child—a little girl. I don't know the details. Her ending wasn't happy. But anyway, that's all in the past. A photograph of you—here—today—should be happy. That's why I want to take one of you as you are now."

"As I am now? What do you mean?"

He didn't know what he meant—or, rather, he did, but wouldn't admit it. It was difficult to be rational. "I mean a photograph of you dressed as you are. Not dressed the way she might have dressed."

"Do I look like her?"

"As you are now—no." It wasn't convincing.

She knew he was being evasive and sensed that in some way he was trying to protect her. From what? From Lowell? Lowell's behaviour—at times almost paranoid—was beginning to have a pattern, and the photograph of the other woman was at the centre of it. Lowell had tried to form her in that woman's image. He had been delighted to the point of euphoria when she had bought the Victorian clothes. He had drooled over her—well, almost—when she wore them. As yet she couldn't see the pattern clearly. This photographer could.

Her hands were cold and there was a dryness at the back of her throat. "In what way was her end sad?"

He wished he could stop the conversation. It should never have reached this stage. "It needn't concern you."

She persisted. "Oh, but I feel it does. Did she die naturally—violently—how?"

He began fiddling with the tripod and didn't answer.

"Was she . . . murdered?" It came out harshly.

He hesitated. It was impossible to fob her off with vague statements—and perhaps unwise. But it was extraordinarily difficult to tell her. The spoken word was somehow too brutal. And so was the written word—but perhaps less so.

He took the photostat copy of the *Illustrated Police News* out of the roll-top desk where he had kept it together with the original photograph, under a pile of old negatives away from his wife's prying eyes. Before handing it to her he glanced at the photograph again. It had been smudged by the photocopier and was by no means as clear as the original. But that, he hoped, would diffuse the shock. The similarity—here—wasn't so striking. The paragraph under it, written in the archaic, florid, pompous prose of the nineteenth century, would have less impact, he hoped, than modern-day reporting of a similar murder. The whole sordid mess would be distanced by its style of presentation.

"A tragedy of the past," he said, handing the paper to Rose. "It occurred more than a hundred years ago. Lowell happened to find the original photograph—somewhere in the cottage, I believe. It has no relevance to either you or him. Read it if you must. And then forget it. It's not the sort of unfortunate affair to commemorate with a fun photograph—if that's what you're trying to do. Had Lowell known the story—what happened to the woman —he wouldn't have wanted you to have the photograph taken in similar style to the other one. Obviously he didn't know its history."

The studio was shaded with heavy blue curtains, and as he drew them back so that she could see to read more easily, a shaft of sunlight struck across her hair. He watched her, moved by her beauty, worried by her growing pallor. He had tried to protect her from what could be a nasty piece of family history, he reminded himself, and she had refused to be protected. Perhaps instinctively. It was better that she should know the truth. An unpleasant truth. But hers was an unpleasant liaison. Possibly dangerous. Certainly damaging. Lowell should bed a woman of his own age and leave this girl alone.

After a few minutes Rose handed the paper back to him. He had thrust her into a nightmare landscape. It had to be walked through. From where? To where? She didn't know.

Leeson waited for her to say something, but she was silent. He asked if the woman's name meant anything to her. "Had you heard of her before?"

She gazed at him blankly, the question not penetrating, and murmured something incoherent.

Perturbed by her reaction, which even in these circumstances seemed extreme, he tried to calm her. "Don't let what you've read upset you. It's past. Finished with. Today's pain is enough for all of us."

Her eyes slowly focused on him as she became aware that he was mouthing words at her—trying to be kind.

"Pain," she repeated the word. And then repudiated it, making little pushing gestures with her hands. "No," she said. *"No!"*

It was some while afterwards when Rose realised that she had left the canvas bag with the maroon dress and necklace behind at the studio. It didn't matter. The dress was only fit for burning. She imagined it on fire in Lowell's garden. Red, the colour of a bloody shroud, as Greg had said. He had been right.

Her footsteps had taken her to the car park—how, she couldn't remember. An hour had gone by—somewhere—like dust in the wind. People were coming and going. Revving engines. Slamming doors. The air smelt of petrol. The bonnet of the Peugeot was cold as she leaned against it trembling. It was impossible to drive home safely—to drive safely anywhere. She needed to be on her own. To sort things out in her head. To rid herself of the nightmare voice that for the first time had spoken clearly and terribly in the full rational light of day.

Ballater received a phone call from Rose at seven o'clock that evening. She wouldn't be returning to the farm for a while, she told him. She wanted to be free to do her own thing—be independent—get a job, perhaps. She would be in touch again when she had an address. He wasn't to worry about her. She was perfectly all right. Quite capable of looking after herself.

The words had come out in a babble and by the time he had gathered his wits and been able to respond she had put the phone down.

Obviously she wasn't perfectly all right.

He had seen her briefly at breakfast and she hadn't seemed disturbed about anything. She was going to Bristol to shop, she'd told him. He had offered to top up the money he had given her before by another twenty pounds and she had accepted with polite reluctance. There was enough money in her savings account to see her through for a while. And she had the car—the small one.

From the practical point of view she could, as she said, look after herself.

But emotionally?

She was eighteen years old—but not eighteen years wise. According to Craddock she still visited Marshall despite all his warnings. He had received the information without comment. Craddock's gratuitous spying, though well-intended, angered him.

After three days of no further contact from her and three sleepless nights of worry, he went down to the cottage.

Lowell, also stressed by Rose's absence, was working on the nocturne. The music reflected his mood and had lost its former tranquillity. The night skies were sombre and starless. The notes on the staves were reluctant to move, but they totally engrossed him. When he went to open the door to Ballater's knock he greeted him without enthusiasm, annoyed by the interruption.

Ballater, relieved to see that he was there, asked if he might come in. "We need to talk."

Lowell apologised. "Of course—I'm sorry." He gestured for Ballater to follow him into the living room and indicated the chair by the empty fireplace.

Ballater noticed the sheets of manuscript on the table and his anxiety abated a little. This talented if washed-up musician wasn't harbouring Rose—though he might know of her whereabouts. He wondered how to question him tactfully.

Lowell, in the real world again where music didn't impinge, was watching him keenly. This wasn't a social call. Growing anxiety overcame discretion. "Is Rose all right?"

Ballater was carefully non-committal. "I believe so—yes."

An odd answer, Lowell thought. He gathered up the music manuscript into a tidy pile and put his pen slantwise across the top. Either she was all right or she wasn't. She hadn't been to see him for nearly a week, but that had happened before when the redheaded lout was staying at the farm. It didn't signify that anything terrible had happened to her. She could have a cold.

She could be growing cold. Even colder.

And that would be terrible for him. An exaggeration? No.

He waited for Ballater to explain himself or to state the reason for his visit.

Ballater was trying to assess the situation objectively. The musician had shown concern and that meant involvement. But he hadn't known of Rose's departure. If—when—she returned, she might return to the cottage and not to the farm. The place had an odd hold on her. And on Marshall. He seemed to be as much part of it as the cold stone floor he was standing on.

As that other man had been . . . over a century ago.

He suppressed the thought. This was a present-day crisis. An unsuitable liaison that must end. To destroy the cottage in order to gain access to the road was desirable. To be rid of Marshall was an even more pressing need.

"I was wondering," he said abruptly, "if you've had second thoughts about selling up?"

Lowell sensed that there was something more to the question than a further sounding-out about a commercial proposition. The old man wanted him out. Primarily because of Rose.

He said he had no intention of leaving.

Ballater glanced critically around him. The cottage now had a very real smell of poverty. The day was chill and there was no sign of a dead fire in the grate or of fresh fuel waiting to be lit. On his last visit he had been given coffee. This time, he guessed correctly, he wouldn't be offered anything.

"I need access," he reiterated. "Don't be afraid of naming a price, even if it seems exorbitant. We can come to an agreement."

"At no price." It was emphatic.

"Why?" The question was sharp, the eyes keen.

"I like being here."

"I find that impossible to believe."

"But it's true."

Ballater shook his head. A fox liked its lair—and this place was little better. A man of Marshall's background wasn't used to squalor—a man of Marshall's background, *if he were totally sane,* would quit.

But the lair was—had been—conveniently near to Rose.

"I'm prepared to double the offer I made last time."

"Sorry—no."

It was time to cut through to the heart of the matter. "Rose has gone. She's no longer at the farm."

Lowell picked up the pencil without being aware of it. It snapped between his fingers. He put the two pieces carefully down on the table. The old man was regarding him as if he were a strange species behind bars. It didn't matter. Let him look. *Don't play games with me. Say what you mean.*

"Gone—where?"

"Bristol initially—she might still be there—I don't know."

Lowell drew out his chair from the table and sat down. A low, ominous buzzing had started inside his head.

"Explain." It was peremptory.

Ballater deliberately waited a moment or two before replying. "The excuse was a shopping trip, but obviously with the intention of not returning. She probably wanted to avoid confrontation by not telling me until after she'd gone. Her phone call was brief—just that she'd contact me when she had an address. That was three days ago, and I haven't heard from her since."

"Have you informed the police?"

"No. She's of age. Free to do as she likes."

"For God's sake, how can you be so complacent?" Lowell's voice was shrill. "Anything could have happened to her."

Whatever had happened to her, Ballater thought bitterly, this gaunt, nerve-ridden, middle-aged man had something to do with it. He could have made her pregnant.

"You may accuse me of anything you like," he answered stiffly, "but not of complacency. I stopped being complacent when Rose was delivered into my care." He glanced towards the window that overlooked the garden. Should he tell Marshall the truth about the cannabis bed?

No, there had been no trouble of that sort recently. Family troubles, and God knew his own had had plenty, were better not discussed. Even so, a few hints about the frailty of Rose's nature might not come amiss.

He phrased it carefully. "Had my wife—her grandmother—been alive when Rose was orphaned she would have given her what she needed—and never received from her own mother—stability—a moral code." It sounded old-fashioned, but he didn't care. Her mother's drug addiction had wrecked the marriage. "Rose came to me when she was fifteen—a difficult age. I sent her to a boarding school—not a very well-chosen establishment, I'm afraid, but I wasn't to know. Some of the friends she made there were undesirable." A mild way of putting it, he thought. Heredity, in Rose's case, had never been well balanced by environment. Even here, in the environs of the farm, there were snares.

He looked coldly at Marshall. "She's immature and lacks judgement. And she won't accept my guidance. I'm concerned only for her good. If she would only realise that, she would have confided in me now."

He moved uncomfortably and his chair scraped against the dusty edge of the grate, dislodging a small carved piece of stone that had been propped against the hearth. Lowell bent down and picked up the fragment of urn, wiping it with the palm of his hand. And then sat holding it.

The question Ballater had to force himself to ask underlined his own failure and it came out gruffly. "I know she has been friendly with you—perhaps spoken freely to you. Can you throw any light on why she should suddenly take off now? Is she in any kind of trouble?" Trouble was Ballater's euphemism for pregnancy. He hoped Marshall understood it.

Lowell did.

He remembered the night when Rose had cried out in her sleep—something about a child. She had sat up in bed, panicked by the nightmare, weeping. He had tried to hold her, comfort her, but she had pushed him away. He had taken no precautions during their love-making but she had assured him that she had that under control. She might have forgotten to protect herself. She could be carrying his child. He felt both guilt and elation.

Ballater noticed Marshall's expression and guessed the conclusion that he had come to. He controlled his anger. Perhaps it was the wrong conclusion. He waited for him to answer and when it became obvious that he couldn't the older man voiced what he hoped was true. "It's possible that she might have gone to the young agricultural student—Farrel—who was here recently. They had quite a warm friendship." If Farrel had got her into trouble, it was easily the less distressing alternative.

Lowell looked briefly into the abyss and then resolutely closed his eyes to it. If Rose was bearing a child, that child was his. When she returned—and she would surely return soon—she would need reassuring and a lot of tender loving. She would also need money—and the stability the old man was talking about. He could provide neither. But must. Somehow. The old man's offer to buy the cottage was tempting, a few thousand pounds could be put to immediate use, but it was an offer he couldn't accept. The money would have to come from another source. This was Rose's place—and his.

He tried to keep his voice level. "I'm sorry, I'm afraid I can't tell you anything. I don't know why Rose has gone. If you should hear from her I'd be obliged if you'd let me know."

Ballater stood up to take his leave. He felt very tired, very aware of his age and inadequacy. The interview had done nothing other than increase his dislike of the musician. There was no obligation to tell him anything. "Thank you for sharing my concern," he said dully. The reply may have been non-committal, but his eyes were decidedly wintry.

TWELVE

If Jane Leeson had been a woman to examine her motives she would have absolved herself from any accusation of spite. She was, she believed, a practical person and a good friend. Lowell's bit on the side had walked out of the studio and left the canvas holdall containing her dress and beads behind. The latter might or might not be valuable, she was no connoisseur of jewellery. If she had also left her name and address they could have been parcelled up and posted to her—but she hadn't. As she hadn't returned for them during the week they would have to be returned to her—via Lowell. The address of Lowell's cottage wasn't known to her either; therefore the holdall would have to be taken to the home once shared by Lowell and Zoe. That was the practical thing to do. The good friend was acting as a good friend should. That was all.

Her husband didn't agree, but couldn't dissuade her. In mitigation he wrote a letter to Lowell and hoped Zoe wouldn't open it.

Drawing a blank at the house was a disappointment. Jane had driven over to Zoe's in happy anticipation of stirring up trouble: the other woman's clothes and beads were tangible evidence of Lowell's love affair. She had prepared sentences of outrage and sympathy and felt cheated of an interesting half hour or so. After ringing the

bell several times she reluctantly pushed her husband's
letter through the letter-box—he had very meanly sealed
it before she could read it—and took the holdall around
to the boiler room at the back of the house. It would be
dry there should it rain. If she hadn't been due at her craft
class at eleven that morning she would have called back
later, but as that wasn't possible she'd phone. She had
behaved very reasonably, she told her husband afterwards. She had done everything that seemed right in the
circumstances. Even her driving as she left Zoe's wasn't to
blame. The other car had skidded into hers and made her
forget the phone call. Who could possibly blame her for
that?

Lowell, driving up the road in the opposite direction,
had witnessed the collision—a minor one—and decided
to do nothing about it. Other drivers had witnessed it,
too, so leave it to them. He hadn't recognised Jane
Leeson; if he had he might have stopped. Or perhaps not.
His social conscience, dulled by a sleepless night, was
now barely alive. In his narrow world there was room
only for Rose. When she came back to him he must present her with a positive plan of action. And for that, Zoe's
co-operation was necessary.

It felt strange to be letting himself into his own house
again. He inserted the key almost furtively and stood in
the small vestibule and smelt the place—floor polish
mixed with the bitter scent of chrysanthemums in a blue
bowl. There was a letter on the mat—a square manila
envelope addressed to him and marked "personal." It assured him of his right to be here and he picked it up and
put it in his jacket pocket before walking through into
the hall with its white doors leading to the reception
rooms. The brass doorknobs gleamed. He felt assailed by
the bright brashness of everything and missed the soft
darkness of the cottage.

It was difficult to believe that he had ever lived here.

Why had he and Zoe, in the first flush of affluence, decided the desirable residence was truly desirable? It looked like a mock-up set in a middle-class soap opera, shining with domestic trivia, very clean. The Chinese rug in the centre of the hall showed no blemish—until he walked on it with his muddy brogues. In the old days he would have felt guilt. The flakes of mud would have been carefully removed and put in the rubbish bin in the kitchen. Now, he looked at them, shrugged, and began a quick tour of the house. It was empty. Frustration mingled with relief. It would have been less harrowing to have got the meeting over quickly; on the other hand, the delay while he awaited her return gave him more time to think and plan.

First, like a thief casing the joint, he went from room to room again and made a mental inventory of his disposable assets. Correction: his and Zoe's disposable assets. Apart from a few ornaments and pictures he had paid for everything. Even if the law allowed it—which it wouldn't —he couldn't leave Zoe bereft of everything except ornaments and pictures. The insurance valuation of the contents was probably lower than it should be in these days of rising prices, but if it could be taken as a guide and the amount split in two, it might be regarded as fair.

Fair to whom? Certainly not to Zoe. She had done nothing wrong—or right. She had entrenched herself in virtue. His was the guilt.

It seemed a mean act to open her wardrobe, but he couldn't resist it. She had covered the mink coat with a nylon overall. Part of the cuff was visible and reminded him of Middy sleeping under the quilt.

It was getting more and more difficult to feed the cat— and to feed himself.

He opened his own wardrobe. Had he ever worn those natty pinstripes? Don't look too hard at that evening suit —your concert get-up—those days have gone. But he still needed shirts and socks and a winter coat. The pigskin suitcase was his; he put it on the bed and filled it with essentials.

The bedroom overlooked the garden. She was keeping it tidy. The borders were neatly raked over and the roses cut back. She was a very efficient woman. He tried to clip his thoughts into shape: that is cold and somehow derogatory. She is your wife, not an automaton who works around the place. And you are hurting her.

He moved away from the window and walked into the adjoining bathroom. He could smell her here—her talc—her soap. It occurred to him that she had always bathed in private—the door locked against him. If, in the future, he could provide Rose with a bathroom she wouldn't be troubled by such inhibitions.

But he could provide Rose with nothing until he had a job. Zoe's efforts to push him into unsuitable employment had been annoying and resistible. But to push himself—for Rose's sake—was different. It was time to get up from what everyone else regarded as the mire and do all the conventional things again. He went along to the study and opened his desk. There were three piles of letters in it, secured with rubber bands. Zoe had written a neat little note on each. *Lowell's. Ours. Mine.* He didn't bother with the *Ours* but quickly flipped through his. Four were circulars—two were reminders that his subscriptions to a book club and the golf club were overdue. He had been too busy with his music composition to miss the books, and even if he could afford to play golf his hands wouldn't let him. The last letter was from his music agent. There was a possibility that a recording of his might be used as theme music for a commercial—if he could come up to London in the near future this could be discussed. The letter was carefully worded—it hinted that the offer might be regarded as a debasement of his talent, but if he were not too sensitive about this he might be prepared to accept the fee, which was negotiable.

The letter was a fortnight old.

He reached for the phone and rang the London office. There was no reply. It took him three or four minutes to realise that this was Saturday and that there was no one there. He would have to wait until Monday to find out if the offer was still open. Whatever it was he would accept it. *Debasement of talent. Sensitive.* Ominous words. The commercial must be pretty crass. But he was beyond caring.

He searched through the desk for various necessary documents that the bureaucratic world would demand to see now that he was returning to it, and took them to the suitcase in the bedroom, together with his agent's letter.

There was a silver cigarette lighter in the desk drawer, he remembered, rarely used now that he'd almost given up. And a gold-plated pen, the one he had once used for signing autographs, a memento of the good days. He went back for them. If he didn't become a telly millionaire turning out musical trash they could be flogged for a few pounds.

The fan who had given him the pen had had L.M. inscribed on it. A Lowell Marshall pen. Was Peterson of the piano factory still trading on his name, he wondered? Or was his name dead?

It was an uncomfortable recollection.

Go and push a few notes on your own piano; there's no one here to wince at the sound you make these days. Try the melody of the nocturne if your hands will let you.

Zoe had put a vase of autumn flowers on the Bechstein. He had warned her never to put anything on it. She could do what she liked with the rest of the house, but the piano was his. He removed the vase and put it on the occasional table next to the wedding photograph. Why was she hanging on to this? He picked it up and scrutinised it. They weren't the same people any more. It was tempting to put it back face down.

When she returned there would be aggro over major matters. Don't make matters worse. Remember the last meeting you had with her. No, for Christ's sake, don't remember it.

He went back to the piano and sat looking at the keys —afraid to play. The nocturne is yours, Rose—an expression of my feeling for you. My fingers can't spell out the words the way I want them to. I'll make a balls-up of it, but I've got to try.

It was like a blind man walking down a familiar corridor. No colour. No light. No shade. A walk that began hesitantly and then gained a little confidence. But not enough. A stumbling, awkward performance. Unfinished. The ending he didn't know until Rose came back to him. And Zoe had had her say.

Zoe, on a day's outing with Ben and Louise to visit their eldest boy at his prep school, was barely aware of the beauty of the Hampshire countryside they were driving through. Ever since they had started the journey Christopher had been chewing barley sugar. Ruining his teeth, she told Louise, who—unwilling to mention travel sickness in Christopher's hearing—hinted there were worse things. Zoe belatedly understood. But surely Ben could have given the child a pill? Doctors tended to dole them out liberally. He was humming to himself as he drove— occasionally contributing to the conversation—a placid, contented family man. Her kind of man. His hands on the steering wheel were square, strong, capable. The kind of hands that got on with everything—a provider's hands. Reassuring. Good to hold. They had touched hers briefly as he had helped her belt herself in. An accidental contact. She wished he'd intended it.

She had a swift unwanted memory of Lowell on the

concert platform in Rome, his fingers rushing over the keys like wild creatures. Assured, brilliant hands. She banished them from her mind and glanced back at Clarissa, who was sleeping peacefully. The two boys took after Louise; the baby was like her father. If she and Lowell had had a child it would have been a strange hybrid, perhaps difficult to love. Gifted, possibly. Unstable, probably. One burden was enough.

The prep school was a fourteenth-century abbey with a modern science block, set amongst trees. As they drove up to the main door Louise tried not to be emotional. Ben had warned her not to baby the boy, especially not in front of anyone. "He'll probably want to shake hands rather than kiss." "Oh, hell and damn," she expostulated, "he's only ten years old." Ben had been nine when he'd gone to the same school, he reminded her. What was he trying to prove, she asked acidly, his ability to survive?

They were to meet the headmaster first, followed by a chat with the housemaster. As Clarissa might wake up and cry, it would be better if Zoe would wheel her around the grounds in her buggy, just for half an hour or so, if she didn't mind. Chris could come along with them, suitably subdued by the scholastic environment, Louise hoped, to be quiet for a while.

Zoe had expected to be put in charge of the baby. It was reasonable. Small boys in grey shirts and pants and red ties were wandering around in groups. A rugby match was in progress. She watched it for a while until the ball came rather close. It was better to move and keep to the garden area. From what Louise told her, this was a middle-income prep school, not one of the gilded establishments. Ben was following family tradition by sending Edward here. Louise hadn't wanted to send him away at all. It was unnatural. Wrong. Ben had won the argument.

Lowell, in the past, had avoided arguments. His favourite word had been "trivial." His favourite phrases:

"Don't bother me." "Do as you like." She hadn't resented his withdrawal into music when his music had won world acclaim. Resentment had grown with his declining ability. Loss of skill should be compensated in other ways. A man like Ben would have met the challenge bravely and with common sense. He wouldn't have walked out on the family.

And got himself someone else.

It was difficult to forget the photograph. The girl had a knowing look. Young, but not innocent. Beautiful and aware of it. Disturbing. Evil. Had he gone kerb-crawling one night and found her? Or had she found him? Would she let him go again now that the kitty was empty? Love, if he deluded himself it was love, couldn't exist on air. No matter what Louise might think of her tactics in dealing with this crisis, she believed she had handled the situation in the best way possible. What else could she have done?

"That's a lovely baby you have there," said a voice at her elbow. The juniors' sports mistress, with sturdy thighs and a too-tight T-shirt, paused on her way over to the rugby field and smiled down at Clarissa, who was sleepily opening her eyes. "Boy or girl?"

"A girl," said Zoe.

"Not one of our future pupils then," the sports mistress laughed. "You must be terribly proud of her."

"Yes," said Zoe. Why bother with explanations? It would have been nice to have been the mother of Ben's child.

When Zoe hadn't returned by midday Lowell went to see if the car was in the garage. It was. So she had gone out with someone. Probably Louise. It was difficult for him to make contact with people these days, even old friends, and he couldn't force himself to go next door and enquire about her.

When things are normal . . . when I know Rose is all right . . . when I'm free of this awful anxiety . . . then I'll feel differently. I'll socialise. Behave like everyone else. Talk a lot of rubbish in the right tone of voice. Smile. Comment on the weather—the garden—politics. Be at ease with myself and others. I don't want this confrontation with Zoe. My instinct tells me to leave. To go now. The cottage is a refuge. It's the only place where I can find peace. The atmosphere in this house is rubbing my nerves raw. But I mustn't quit. For Rose's sake, I have to stay and wait.

It occurred to him that he hadn't eaten. His appetite these days was small and he could tell by his clothes that he had lost weight. If you reduced your intake your stomach adjusted. Which was just as well. But there was food here, and it would pass the time to cook it.

When he rooted around the kitchen he was amazed at the amount of food she had stored. Apart from the essentials, there was a lot of luxury stuff: pâté de foie gras, smoked salmon, tins of continental delicacies he'd never heard of and didn't want to try. What was she preparing for? A banquet? A siege? Did she know that one day he'd come along and look? And make comparisons? What did she expect him to do? Beg for famine relief?

Well—why not? But don't beg. Take.

There was a large cardboard box on the floor next to the fridge. It was full of china. A Royal Doulton tea service with a delicate floral pattern and still packed in white tissue paper. New. When was she going to stem the financial flow? Or had she bought this, and all the surplus food, when there had been money in the joint account? Probably.

His temper was rising as he unpacked it. One of the plates dropped and broke into two neat sections. He kicked them to one side. The empty box was a convenient size and he filled it with essentials—and a few non-essentials. He reminded himself to include food for the cat: several tins of meat and a couple of bottles of fresh milk.

There was steak in the lower section of the fridge, also bacon and sausages. He made himself a mixed grill, something he hadn't had for a long time, and followed it with real coffee.

He had forgotten that you ate food politely, slowly, and that overindulgence made you queasy. Before he'd started cooking it he thought he wasn't hungry. But he'd eaten too much. Too fast.

The cardboard box would have to be carried out to the van before she came back. To struggle out with it while she watched would be conceding her victory in a minor battle—undignified. Dignity. Indignity. Words he never thought of in the cottage. It was heavier than he expected, and he had to remove the milk bottles and some of the tins and make a separate journey with them. The van was capacious and he decided to fill up the space with a couple of sacks of fuel. There were half a dozen in the boiler room, he discovered, so take three. Leave three for Zoe. It was when he was about to remove them that he saw Rose's holdall. Jane had wedged it unobtrusively between two of the bags.

At first he couldn't believe it was hers. A lot of people had canvas holdalls. He hadn't noticed it particularly when they had gone shopping together. Curiosity prompted him to look inside.

The maroon dress was neatly folded, and the coral necklace carefully pinned to the bodice with a large safety pin. In such a way are the clothes of the dead put away for disposal. Made irrational by shock, he stood and looked at them and believed that something terrible had happened to her.

Had happened to her here.

THIRTEEN

For Zoe, the day's outing had been reasonably pleasant. Eddie had pleased his mother by kissing her. Had kissed them all, in fact. He had pleased both parents by being obviously happy. The child wasn't wilting in an alien environment. They had lunched together at a small restaurant full of pseudo-oak beams and bright red table-cloths. The afternoon was spent in Winchester wandering around the shops and going to the cathedral. Ben showed the boys the mortuary chests containing the remains of Canute, and Christopher had shouted, "Get back sea! Get back sea! You're making my feet wet!" Eddie, suddenly very grown up and self-conscious, had hissed at him to shut up. "Don't be such a *child.*" Louise and Ben had smiled at each other and Zoe had felt excluded. Later, when it was time to take Eddie back to school, Louise had kissed him at the gate and his father had walked up to the main door with him. Louise's eyes had filled with tears and she had gripped Zoe's arm hard. "I'm glad you came."

On the whole, Zoe thought, she was glad, too. But she wouldn't be sorry to get home. Eddie had become a very civilised child. Christopher wasn't. He didn't want to sit on Louise's knee on the drive back. He wanted to sit in the front on Zoe's knee. Zoe pretended not to hear him.

She was wearing a tweed check suit in shades of lovat green and brown and she didn't want his sticky fingers on it—or worse. He had eaten an assortment of sweets during the afternoon, followed by an ice-cream, and was now into barley sugar again. Louise told him that young children weren't allowed in the front of cars. Annoyed, he had reached across Ben and tried to touch the steering wheel and Ben had slapped his hand lightly. "Do you want to kill your loving family?"

That anyone should want to kill anyone on this tender lovely evening was a concept beyond the understanding of all of them. The sky was darkening into a grey mother-of-pearl. Clarissa, half awake but contented, was murmuring to herself. Christopher had at last gone to sleep and Louise, her chin resting gently on his head, was thinking of the son who wasn't with her.

She was the first to notice the yellow van as they drove up the adjoining drive—and felt a surge of very real pleasure. The prodigal, if he could be called that, had returned. Zoe wouldn't be going into a lonely house after the razzmatazz and bother and warmth of a normal family.

"Look," she said.

Zoe stiffened. She had been imagining this meeting for some time. Always differently. Sometimes he was contrite. Sometimes aloof. Always a little frightening. Their last confrontation in the cottage was unforgettable.

She sounded calmer than she felt. "It seems Lowell's come back."

"Not before time," Louise said, "but welcome."

Ben drew up the car and then glanced at Zoe. His wife was assuming rather too much. He asked Zoe if she wanted him to go in with her. "But I have to phone the hospital first."

"Bring him round for drinks after I've got the kids to

bed," Louise suggested. "That is, if you want to. Do what you think is best."

"I'd better see him on my own."

Zoe stood in the driveway and looked at her home next door. Lights were on in all the rooms facing the front, and the curtains were drawn. She had never imagined the meeting in the evening when the garden was dark with shadows and the air cold with the coming of night. Shivering a little, she fumbled for her key and went towards the front door.

Lowell had had too long to think and his thoughts were tortuous. He had walked a labyrinth with no known exit. Rose, destroyed in some way he couldn't understand, was at the centre of it. She had been here, he believed, inveigled, tricked into coming. But how? Why? It wasn't in her nature to seek an interview with Zoe. If she was bearing his child, Zoe was the last person she'd tell. Or was she? Had he misunderstood her nature completely? Had she come to sound out Zoe's reaction? He couldn't believe it. She would have told him. So why had she come?

Why were her clothes here?

Where the hell was she?

In the first hour after finding her dress and necklace he might have been prepared to accept a rational explanation —or even a bemused denial of involvement. But as time had gone on he had found it necessary to try to calm himself. A measure of scotch helped. A second measure had him pacing the house again. A third took him into the garden, where he looked at the neat undisturbed flower-beds. He told himself he was behaving like a fool, that his suspicions were groundless, but he didn't believe what he told himself any more.

The enigma grew more ugly as darkness fell.

He needed lights everywhere and went around the house switching them on. And then he went and sat on the blue dralon chair in the immaculate drawing-room, the bottle of scotch at his side, Rose's dress draped carefully along the sofa as if she were in it and alive.

He didn't hear Zoe letting herself in.

But he sensed she was standing at the door looking at him.

Her first words, spoken without thought and due to extreme nervousness, were unwise. "You've been drinking."

He didn't answer. She was recognisable as a stranger one passes occasionally in the street. It was impossible to persuade himself that he had cohabited with this woman —that they had slept together—eaten together—planned their lives together. That's your wife standing there, Lowell, you'd better believe it. The woman in the wedding photograph. The woman who knows about Rose.

She took a step into the room and noticed a dark red dress on the sofa. On the arm of the sofa was a coral necklace. At first she didn't associate them with Jane Leeson's description. What were they? Peace offerings? A new gown. Totally unsuitable. Coral. Probably fake. What was she supposed to do? Exclaim rapturously, "Oh Lowell, how kind, welcome back to the fold?"

He was watching her watching the dress.

She didn't know what to do or say and wished he would do or say something to break the silence. Was he expecting to stay the night? If so she didn't want to sleep with him. Should she offer him something to eat? Or black coffee—which he probably needed. Would that be tactless as her first remark had, in retrospect, been tactless? She had done everything in her power to force him back and now knew quite clearly and definitely that she didn't want him. Not like this.

"Well," she taunted foolishly, "it has been a long time."

She made a vague gesture towards the necklace. A

comment of some sort seemed to be expected. But what? He'd returned with a bauble—some expensive beads.

"Don't!" He thought she was about to touch them.

Beads. Jane Leeson's description. A long old-fashioned maroon-coloured dress. He'd brought his whore's clothes here. Shocked, she looked him fully in the eyes for the first time.

He saw in her face what he expected to see. "So you know Rose."

Who? No one had put a name to the woman before. "If you're talking about your . . ." She had been about to say *whore* but bit it back.

"My what?"

"I don't know—whoever you've been associating with."

"Don't pretend you don't know her. She's been here."

What was the matter with him? He must be more drunk than she'd thought. Or crazier. "Why should she come here?"

"That's what I want to know. You tell me."

Dear God, she thought, I don't know how to handle this. She shook her head mutely.

"She's been here. You put her dress and the necklace in the boiler room. What were you going to do with them— burn them?"

"I don't know what you're talking about."

"Yes, you do, Zoe. And you've got to tell me." He tried to make his voice sound reasonable.

The smooth tones had the silky menace of an inquisitor intent on a confession. But she had nothing to confess.

"Her clothes in the boiler room? I honestly don't know what you mean."

"They were in a canvas bag. You'd folded the dress and pinned the coral necklace to it."

She supposed she should humour him but she didn't know how. "You've been drinking and you're talking a lot of rubbish. I'll get you some coffee. We'll talk again when you can tell me sensibly what you're on about."

She'd make for the kitchen, she thought, and let herself out through the back door. Ben was needed here.

Lowell, reading guilt in her every movement, followed her swiftly. She wasn't getting away. They stood together in the kitchen—he with his back to the door, blocking her exit. "You've got to tell me how you got her to come here —what you said to her—what she said to you—*what happened to her.*"

She felt hysteria rising. It was like a mad game of Consequences at a macabre party. What was she supposed to have done to this unknown bitch? Open up the last bit of paper and all will be revealed.

In an effort to quell the hysteria she made herself do ordinary things—putting the kettle on to boil—milk to warm—instant coffee in two brown mugs. But to Lowell her apparent indifference was infuriating. "Stop it! Answer me!" He moved towards her and she backed away, smiling foolishly, her body bathed in sweat.

"Lowell—I don't understand. How can I answer you when I don't understand?"

"Stop lying to me. She came here and you . . ."

"No! No! No! I've been out all day. I don't know who . . ."

"Not today. Recently. What happened to her? By Christ, if you've hurt her . . . if you've . . ."

The threat, unspoken, terrified her. She began babbling at him in an attempt to diffuse his anger. He wasn't well, she told him. Everything would work out. In the meantime, be sensible. They should have got together before. It wasn't too late now to—well, to try to . . . oh, God, to be *calm.*

He watched her, his eyes glazed. Her mouth was opening and closing, spewing words at him that failed to make any contact in his mind. She seemed unsubstantial, fleshless, a long way off, while the kitchen seemed to close in on him and then recede to the accompaniment of a thumping in his head like a primitive drumbeat.

He moved closer to her. *"Where is Rose?"* The shouted question seemed to him little more than a whisper. She cringed back from him, pressing herself against the stove, wondering if she could edge past and make for the door. She took a couple of tentative steps but he reached out and swiftly held her by the shoulders. Contact with her brought him a brief feeling of reality. The voice of reason, speaking clearly over the cacophony in his head, warned him to back off. To stop. He almost heeded it.

She felt his fingers digging into her shoulders, relaxing slightly and then gripping more strongly so that she couldn't move. She felt weak. Helpless. No words could be clawed out of the air to calm him.

He was asking again. "Where is she? What happened here? Where is Rose?"

She lost control finally and screamed at him in panic. "I don't know where the bloody bitch is . . . I don't know . . . I don't know!"

There was a hissing sound of milk boiling over on the stove behind her and she managed to twist herself sideways and grab the saucepan. Her aim, intended to catch him full in the face with the boiling liquid, was inhibited by the way he was holding her, but some of it splashed his cheek.

The sudden scalding pain, unexpected and acute, thrust him into a vortex of uncontrollable rage. His distorted hands were clumsy about her throat and this time as she struggled, kicking and gasping, it was skin on skin, not a fantasy attack that did no harm. He squeezed with all his strength, pushing her down onto the floor, while a raucous parody of the nocturne played fortissimo in his head.

·   ·   ·   ·

Lowell had no recollection of leaving the house some while later and getting into the van. There was a blank period of no memory, like a black dreamless sleep, followed by a slow awakening to events too horrific to contemplate. So don't think. Just be.

He was sufficiently sober by now to know that it was necessary to drive with extra care—but not to appear too careful. It wouldn't do to be breathalysed. His emotions were slotted into different compartments, and he locked up those that might get in the way of a safe drive back to the cottage. He was aware of traffic hazards in the environs of Bristol and stretches of hazardous road in the Gloucestershire countryside. He was conscious of feeling cold in the van and of the unpleasant smell of petrol. The windscreen de-mister wasn't working and he had to strain to see.

Get home, he told himself. Concentrate.

He didn't allow himself to think about Zoe until he arrived at the field entrance to the cottage. And the thought was incoherent. Something about the great sweep of the night sky. A disbelief in mortality. Remorse was a physical ache. Inexpressible.

As he got out of the van he heard a soft purring and felt the warm caress of a cat rubbing his legs. Middy, lonely, had come to welcome him home. He picked him up and held the animal close. Needing love. Giving it. The cat wasn't the bony creature it had been when Rose had first given it to him. It was long and lean and hungry. He suddenly remembered the food in the van.

"Tonight," he told it, "you'll eat."

In the light of the torch he removed some of the luxury items from the cardboard box and put in the milk. It was tempting to take one of the sacks of fuel up to the cottage and have one last night of heat—a temptation he couldn't resist. By half emptying one of the sacks onto the floor of the van he found he could drag it with his right hand and hold onto the box with his left. With the torch balanced on the box he could see where he was going.

The word "survival" came into his mind. The cottage was a sanctuary. If he could reach it and not drop anything . . . if the cat would stay away from his feet. . . .

The fuchsia by the broken-down gate spilled a few dead blossoms as he brushed past it. The weeds on the path, crisp with frost, were slippery white hummocks in the darkness leading to the door. He eased down the sack of fuel, put the box beside it, and felt for his key. The familiar smell of the cottage soothed him as he opened the door.

Make a fire, he told himself. Light candles. Get a big, bright blaze going. There's no need to be careful with the small hoard of wood any more. Use it all. Why not?

He banked it up in the grate, added a little lighter fuel, and carefully built a pyramid of coal on top of it. He lit a candle and then lit the fire with the candle flame. As the fire took hold, the walls of the cottage danced with saffron-coloured shadows. He found more candles, a dozen unused in a box. No holders for all of them. Then use anything—mugs—egg-cups—put them on a tray to catch the drips.

Light. There had to be light.

Lastly, he unpacked the cardboard box and arranged the tins and packets on the table. The tins of sardines, salmon and corned beef he pushed to one end of it. Those were Middy's. The rest was just food that he could look at and not want.

Middy, getting impatient, was miaowing with hunger. "All right," he said testily, "all right—all *right!*"

He took the tin of sardines through to the lean-to, opened it, and emptied the contents onto the cat's dish. Middy pushed through his legs as he stooped, almost unbalancing him. "Damn you, take it easy!"

He had a sudden compulsion to wash his hands in hot

water, but couldn't find matches to light the stove. He felt
in his pocket for his lighter and his fingers touched the
hard squareness of an envelope. Suddenly the events of
the last few hours gripped him in a violent despairing
spasm. Almost operating on remote control, he removed
it, looked at it, and remembered finding it on the mat in
that other house in that other lifetime. Once more it gave
him a feeling of identity, but this time it wasn't reassuring. It was better to be a non-person. To cease.

He washed his hands, trying to ignore the letter. Extinction was an impossible concept. His body was uncomfortably alive. His hands tingled. And there was a
blister on his cheek where the boiling milk had splashed
him.

If she hadn't done that . . .

If she had stayed calm . . .

If I . . . if I . . .

He had been sitting by the fire for some time before he
decided to open the letter.

Leeson had protected the photograph with two thin
pieces of white cardboard held with an elastic band. The
note, penned on a large sheet of paper, had been slipped
under the band and not folded.

There was no greeting—just an uneasy scrawl:

I'm sorry if landing you with the girl's clothes is an
embarrassment. She left them at the studio when she
called and I haven't her name or address. Jane and I are
off to Italy—a photographic assignment—otherwise we
would have held on to them a while longer. Jane
promises to give Zoe a tactful explanation. As she's not
brilliantly inventive I don't know what she'll say.
We've had a running argument about this, but as I
didn't know the address of your cottage either, I
couldn't think of an alternative course of action. We'll

be away until the twenty-seventh. Come and see me in
the studio any time after that and I'll present you with
a couple of bottles of duty-free in compensation for
any hassle.

You'll find enclosed the original photograph you
brought me some time ago—the one I took the
enlargement from. I would have returned it to you
before, but the information I dug up about it was
disturbing, to say the least. My reaction—rather
cowardly—was to shove it in a drawer and try to forget
it. Her name was Anne-Marie Tarrant. If you haven't
already heard the details of her background I'll fill you
in on this when we meet.

He'd signed the note with his initials: E.L.

Lowell, too emotionally mind-blown to try to make
any sense of the first part of the letter, was immediately
thrust into action by the second paragraph. He took the
elastic band off the two pieces of cardboard, and there
neatly coffined between them was Rose. His delightful,
beautiful, un-dead wonderful girl. He felt the same surge
of excitement, the same strong sexual awareness, he had
felt when he had first held this sepia photograph in the
early days of the summer. The lips were amused—and
now he knew their taste, their texture. The eyes were
intently probing—a remembered deep, dark blue. The
voice—her voice was speaking his name softly in the familiar accent. Time was a confusion, a strange blending of
Then and Now. He touched her face very tenderly and
believed he felt warm flesh. And almost wept with pleasure.

A brief scanning of the second paragraph, once again,
took a little of the shine away. Anne-Marie Tarrant? That
was nonsense. Leeson had got it wrong. "Disturbing, to
say the least." What the hell was he on about? This was
Rose. Perfect in her imperfection.

Before the letter could contaminate him with reason, he pushed it into the fire and watched it burn.

For a long time he held the photograph, fingering it gently, careful not to mark it, and then he pinned it to the corkboard on the wall. As before he felt the need of a larger portrait of her, as large as the one Zoe had destroyed. She had viciously torn the eyes, he remembered.

An eye for an eye, Zoe. My guilt feels less as I remember that.

A few words from Leeson's letter drifted into his mind —a girl's clothes left at the studio—what girl? Rose? But why? Something about an address. He should have kept the letter. Read it more calmly. It seemed to be offering an explanation about something. But whatever it was, it was too late.

He took the tins of food through to the lean-to and piled them up on the draining board. Then he returned to the living-room and pushed the table up against the wall under the portrait.

Assemble all the candles so that the light shines on her. It's a gentle light, candle-light. I can see her smiling at me through it.

He angled his chair so that he could sit by the fire and watch her. Her presence would help him through the waiting hours of the night. The police would have to be told about Zoe's murder tomorrow, but tonight he had a few hours of peace. The cat jumped on his knee and as he stroked its fur he could feel its heart beating very fast, almost imperceptibly, like the quiet ticking of a clock.

FOURTEEN

"Pot is one thing," Greg said, "but I'm not into mind-benders."

"Cheap," Rose replied, quoting the pusher. "The price of a few gallons of petrol and you're off to paradise."

They were sitting on the bed in Greg's second-floor flat in Gloucester. Downstairs the party they had just left was rocking the building. This new Rose who had descended upon him had joined the gaudy throng, for reasons she wouldn't divulge, and had lost some of her individuality. War-painted like the rest of them, she merged with the subculture.

He hadn't wanted a punk girlfriend.

He wanted Rose.

She sensed his disapproval and didn't care. At this point of crisis she couldn't bear a quiet limbo. She had to declare herself loudly, brashly. A change of appearance was like hanging a net over a mirror; she had the same eyes but consoled herself by looking at herself differently. This is who I am. How I am. This is me, *now.* I am myself, damn you!

She had driven over to him after the metamorphosis had been completed to her satisfaction—not just the punk hair-do, short, spiky, crimson-dyed and outrageous —and the make-up, orange domino mask and a curve of ochre on the cheeks—but clothes, too, tight, tarty, as far removed from the Victorian image as possible. She hadn't expected him to greet her with ecstatic joy—his emotions weren't extreme like Lowell's, thankfully—but neither had she expected a degree of embarrassment.

It was, she discovered, easier to look the part than to feel it. The tablets should help.

Rose held two of them on the palm of her hand. "One for you—one for me."

She had stayed a few days in a cheap hotel near the Bristol docks, too bruised mentally to contemplate going anywhere. Eventually, forced out by the need to buy basic necessities, she had met the pusher in the toilets in one of the big stores. She had always imagined drug pushing to be a male-dominated business and had been surprised when the prim-looking blonde in a navy blue duffel coat had approached her. The woman's sixth sense, or whatever radar she operated by, had homed straight in and the deal had been made without hassle.

Greg, relieved that the acid hadn't been obtained locally, nevertheless wasn't happy. He had never had direct contact with the pushers—the students who bought dope shared it—and if it wasn't offered him, he did without.

"You took a hell of a risk."

She shrugged. "They're smoking grass downstairs—that's risky, too."

"Does your grandfather know you're here?"

"I'll phone him tomorrow—if I decide to stay."

Her assumption that he wanted her to stay was correct, despite obvious difficulties. An occasional girl-friend called Gail was one of them. A shared bathroom with three other male students—all predatory—was another.

"Why did you come?" He had asked it before and her answer had been evasive.

It still was. "Thank you for your enthusiastic welcome."

"I'm glad to have you."

"By the look of you—overjoyed." It was tart.

"I mean it—flush those tablets down the bog—and come to bed with me."

She gestured impatiently. "I need to get away—inside my head—afterwards I'll—I can't now—I don't want you now." (When you touch me I think of Lowell. I've got to blot him out. Extinguish him. Make him go.)

He was perceptive enough to know that she was suffering from some sort of emotional wound that had nothing to do with him. With Marshall, perhaps? If the weirdo had kicked her out, well and good. She had come to him, even better. So give her time.

There was a crash downstairs as someone knocked the record player over. This was followed by a few minutes of silence. Then the music started up again.

The LSD tablets were two tiny blobs on the palm of her hand. "I suppose we should take them with water." Rose went over to the washbasin and rinsed out a tumbler. There were traces of toothpaste in it. She rinsed it again and held it out to him.

"No," he said.

"Please." Her voice was cajoling. "It will be lonely out there without you."

It was crazy and dangerous. Afterwards he couldn't justify his weakness in giving in and didn't try. It was the most extraordinary sensory experience he had ever had and one he never wanted to repeat. There was no substance in the bed as he lay pressed up against Rose. The wall at his back flowed around him with the softness of feathers. He believed that he got up and felt his feet sink through the floor while the music from down below came up like vapour and was breathed rather than heard. He yearned for something hard to hold, but there was nothing solid anywhere. All was soft, viscous, sour-smelling.

He clutched his arms, but his fingers went through flesh
as if he were a drowned man coming apart in a terrible
dissolution. As the effect of the acid slowly wore off, his
body, like a film run backwards from death to life, became hard again. He could feel the bones of his legs, his
arms, his fingers, as his skeleton reassembled.

His re-creation—like the creating of Adam on the first
day—had taken a little time. The party down below was
over. The room was silent and dark. He had been away
for some hours. If Rose's experience had been the same,
he thought kindly, she would need one of his ribs to
stiffen her. He offered her one, very seriously, in the
darkness. She didn't reply. He reached out to feel her. She
wasn't there.

The suburban road, narrow and deserted, seemed to
stretch onwards towards a narrow cone of light that never
enlarged, never diminished. Rose, exhausted with running, slackened her pace a little and took in long gulps of
air. At last she had breath enough to say what had to be
said. "I didn't kill my baby. It was a foetus—a few cells—
not yet a baby. It felt nothing."

The nurse, somewhere unseen in the night, disposed of
the bloodied remains, also unseen. Her voice, though
barely above a whisper, was clear. "Abortion is murder."

Rose began running again, her footsteps irregular like
terrified heartbeats. "I was fourteen—too young—the
doctor agreed. It felt nothing. *Nothing.*"

It was necessary to keep on repeating this. The words
went around in circles like a hoop being bowled down a
corridor—a long corridor of whitewashed walls—and
with a door at the end of it.

The door must remain closed.

Beyond it was pain.

A long fall into darkness.

The accusing voice was changing, assuming a different

timbre resonant with menace. The charge wasn't murder of an unborn child. There would be no donning of a black cap for a promiscuous fourteen-year-old. She was a woman now, responsible for her actions. It was murder of the first degree. She had killed in cold blood.

"But *who?*" she screamed. *"Who?"*

The question, unanswered, reverberated as if her skull were a cavern full of a roaring sea. The sea, like tears, was warm on her face. There were rats in the water, swollen-bellied, drowned. When the sea reached the top of the cave . . . into her nostrils . . .

She took a shuddering gasp of breath.

That happened to Alice. Her father was reading her the story, a long time ago. And briefly was with her now: "Stop weeping, Rose. Alice didn't drown. She grew. Her neck was distorted—like a snake."

She turned to him for comfort. He wasn't there.

You're running down a long silent street. Alone. The shadows are like black pits and the gaslight is too bright. Bright as the sun. But it's night. Half night—half day. But which?

They said dawn.

How will I know dawn when it comes? The light is on all night. So how will I know?

Keep running—as the world tilts towards the day, run faster. Make it stay dark—force it to stay night always—don't let the morning come.

She was running wildly when the two college students saw her and recognised her from the party as Greg's girl-friend. They guessed she was on a bad trip and moved in swiftly before she could hurt herself. She felt their hands holding her firmly and one of them pushed his scarf over her mouth to muffle her scream.

She felt she was dying.

They knew she was passing out.

They half carried her back to Greg's flat, which was a

couple of streets away. If this was goddamned mescaline, or whatever, she was unlikely to use it again. Greg, they discovered, was mind-blown, too, but gradually normalising, so it was their duty to stay around. It was easier to put Rose on the sofa in the party room after they'd kicked the debris out of the way than to get her upstairs. They sat and watched her while Greg paced the room with exaggeratedly heavy footsteps.

"The world," he said, smiling foolishly, "is hard."

"Too bloody right it is," they agreed.

Rose, hearing them through thick heavy darkness, was afraid to open her eyes. She didn't know where she was and she longed to be back in the cottage where it was safe. She spoke with her eyes tightly closed.

"I want to go home," she said.

The candles began to gutter at a little after 3 A.M. Lowell, vaguely aware that the light wasn't as strong as it had been, stopped fighting sleep and dozed a little. Middy snuggled up closer to him, his shadow a small lump on Lowell's shadow on the ancient walls, so that they seemed to merge like a grotesque pregnancy.

Rose couldn't rationalise her urge to return to the cottage. She couldn't rationalise anything. She felt as if she were suspended over a chasm between a past that was dark and terrifying and a future that inexorably beckoned. She had gone away to escape Lowell, but the cottage was part of both of them and it was demanding her presence. She had to be there—and soon.

It was something to do with innocence. And an accusation she didn't understand.

The two students who were watching over her told her very sensibly that if she tried to drive the car she'd probably kill herself. When Greg offered to drive her they gave him a similar warning.

During the last half hour or so she had been pacing the
room like a caged animal, insisting that the door should
be kept ajar and the window opened wide. No, she said,
she wasn't claustrophobic. Well—not usually. In her trip
she had been in too small a room—that was all.

The trip, one of her keepers told her, might linger a bit.
Acid did odd things to your mind. Driving a car through
the dawn wasn't on. Wait a few hours. Preferably wait a
whole day.

A whole day was too long—even a few hours would be
too late. She couldn't explain this so didn't try.

"I have to go home."

Greg saw "home" as the farm—and Ballater. He was
still too confused for any sort of confrontation with the
old man. When he tried to construct a few sentences in
his mind—excusing himself—excusing Rose—they didn't
sound lucid. He'd been smashed on booze once or twice,
but this was different. Booze was soporific; the brain was
programmed to zero, it curled up and slept. Acid was a
mad flock of birds that couldn't be cajoled to roost—until
they were ready.

"I don't think I'm entirely with it," he said placidly,
"and neither are you, Rose. You might put the accelerator
through the floor."

An insubstantial floor, he recalled, with the quality of
sponge rubber. He rephrased it: "You might drive too
fast."

A southeasterly breeze carried the sound of church bells
towards the cottage. Lowell had heard them a few times
before on the Sundays when life was normal and they
were just background music at the commencement of an
ordinary day.

In many ways this day felt ordinary, too.

Bodily functions went on. He walked down the garden
to the privy and noticed that his shoes were wet with

dew. A spider had spun a web between a spade and the wall it leaned against. Nature, in a teasing mood, flung small dead leaves around. He felt one in his hair and removed it. It was brown and crisp. Clean.

Trees managed the business of dying very well. They went out in a blaze of glory. Flowers decayed, and so did people.

Before leaving the privy he disinfected it with pine fluid. A misnomer. A pine forest smelt of green sap rising —of a floor of rugged cones on wet sweet earth.

It would be pleasant on this cold sharp morning to stroll across the fields and listen to the bells.

So why not do so?

Because this day is like no other. When the bells stop ringing you must plan your next move.

Words his father had spoken to him shortly before he died came to him: "Everything is in order, Lowell. You'll find all the necessary papers in a series of manila envelopes in the top right-hand drawer of the bureau." An extremely simple filing system.

Lowell returned to the cottage and stood looking at the portrait of Rose. He had no file. No manila envelopes. No desire to tidy up his life so that it could be handed over to someone else.

He had the unfinished nocturne and the portrait.

If they—whoever they might be—tried to take either from him he would kill them.

It was a statement of fact—a very cool assertion of intent.

FIFTEEN

Rose drew up her car behind Lowell's van at the precise moment the bells stopped.

She had no clear recollection of the journey. All she could remember was the coldness. She had driven with the windows rolled down and the wind had whipped around the interior of the car, chilling her hands, her ankles. To be enclosed was unbearable. It was better to freeze than suffocate. Remnants of the terror of the acid trip still trailed across her thoughts like an unravelling rope. Until she was free of the memory she couldn't think clearly. That she should have arrived safely at her destination was due, she believed, to well-trained reflexes. And luck. She was in no state to question the nature of the luck. She was here because she had to be.

There were wide fields all around, shimmering silver-green in the morning sun. Clouds sailed briskly across the deep blue of the sky. Freedom was a simple matter of breathing, moving.

She saw as she approached the cottage that a dark curl of smoke was coming from the single chimney. Lowell's presence was unacceptable, but for a while had to be accepted. He had intruded on her domain—taken over her place. They had loved sexually and that had been good—until he had tried to twist her into something she wasn't.

And left her not knowing who or what she was.

In coming here now she was searching for her identity, though she didn't put it to herself like that. She was Rose, she kept telling herself. And didn't wonder at the need to be told. This was the last part of the twentieth century. And so? The acid trip had been timeless. It didn't slot into history anywhere. So why this strong feeling of the past? A feeling that was getting stronger as she walked down the path to the door.

"Deadlines may be set, they can also be ignored," She said. For quite some time now, she had learnt the knack of talking to him inside his head—or perhaps it was he who had learnt the knack of listening to her. Her expression, amused, smiling, didn't visibly change. They were back to the old relationship, the one before she became flesh. They had discussions then, too, but the merging of minds hadn't been quite so complete. He sensed her rising dominance now, a dominance he welcomed. Since killing Zoe he had been unsure what to do. When the bells stopped—and they just had—he was supposed to do something—but what? Her answer was clear and consoling.

He remembered he'd brought a bottle of scotch from the house and that it was in the cardboard box in the lean-to. He went through and poured some into a tumbler—not too much—and added water. He saw it as a celebratory drink—a successful passing of a deadline. But murder wasn't celebratory. When he couldn't see the portrait on the wall his more sombre thoughts obtruded. It was like walking from light to shade.

"Lowell!" The voice was very distinct. Pleased to be recalled to the light, he obeyed it.

And saw the stranger. The parody.

Rose had let herself in quietly and was crouching by the fire warming herself. Her thighs were goose-pimpled where the slit in her black velvet skirt exposed them. Her fingers, paining in the sudden warmth, were gradually becoming a more normal colour. She hadn't washed her face since painting it for the party and the tears she had wept during the crazy terror of the trip had melted the orange mask around her eyes so that it trailed grotesquely over her cheeks. Her hair, wind-battered, spiked around her head in bloodied spears. She had no idea how she looked and couldn't understand Lowell's silence. He was standing by the door staring at her as if she were an apparition.

She told him sharply that she had been driving for a long time and that she was cold. "At least you have a good fire going for once—and I could do with something hot to drink."

Her voice was Rose's voice. Her features were Rose's features made grotesque. Words of Leeson's when he had first seen the photograph came to him. He had said she looked like a whore. This creature looked like a whore. Her red satin blouse was split almost to the navel.

She saw the direction of his glance. "Yes," she agreed, "a stupid way to dress on a cold day, but I came in a hurry. I had to get here."

She noticed that his hand holding the glass of whisky trembled and wondered if he was stoned. Or was that too simple an explanation? In the few days since they had seen each other he had changed subtly. His eyes weren't Lowell's eyes as she remembered them, warm with love for her. Her own brash declaration of self was a pale posturing compared to the change in him. She sensed trauma deeper than her own.

She spoke his name, making it a question: "Lowell?"

He looked to the photograph on the wall for guidance, but there was a blank silence inside his head. He walked across the room and put the glass of whisky down on the table. The candles had burnt out and he placed them in a neat row on the tray. If he did things with his hands, his brain might start working again. He didn't know how to deal with the situation. Words were required of him, but he didn't know what they should be.

Rose, to break the silence, asked him how his hands were.

Strong enough for killing, he remembered. He disturbed the row of candles, rearranging the pattern. His bloody hands!

"Lowell! Why the hell don't you talk to me?"

Echoes of the old Rose. Memories surfaced. He had undressed her by the fire: her long hair had shone in the light from it.

"What have you done to your hair?" He was standing half turned from her, mumbling the question.

"I've cut it," she said crisply, "as you can see."

Her mind, fogged by the acid, was clearing and she became aware of the odd way he had arranged the room. He seemed to have made a crypt of it. What was the purpose of pushing the table up against the wall? With all the spent candles on it it looked like a crude little altar. The focal point was a small sepia photograph.

She got up and went to see it closer.

Recognition was followed by a hot anger that made her heart thud. This was the original portrait. The one that the photographer had talked about. It was much clearer than the one in the *Illustrated Police News.* Here the resemblance was so strong she could be looking at her mirror image. But the eyes were different, she told herself. Different. Whatever went on behind the eyes of that woman of long ago wasn't mirrored in hers now.

I am not you, she told the photograph silently.

I wasn't accused of stabbing my lover to death. And our child. Our month-old infant son. Oh, Christ! What kind of a monster would that make me? Make you? *You.* I wasn't taken, sick and terrified, to that terrible room on that awful morning. And hanged by my neck until I was dead. It was *you*. Not me. *You*.

The smile of the other woman was quizzical.

Rose turned away, shaking.

"You tried to make me into that."

"That is Rose."

"Don't be so goddamned stupid." She didn't know whether to hit him or to cry.

He told her gently to sit down, that he'd get her the hot drink she'd asked for earlier. "There's no need to be distressed about anything."

The words were coming into his head very easily now, as if a prompter backstage was feeding him the right lines. This grotesque little travesty should be handled kindly, he sensed, until he knew more about her.

She wasn't sure if she could trust his change of mood. It was too quick, too suave. His eyes had a shuttered look to them as if he were wary of revealing his thoughts.

Her own thoughts were becoming more disciplined. The LSD had made her feel guilty on account of the abortion. The nurse's words, overheard when she had been too lightly sedated, about abortion being murder, had always troubled her. Given her nightmares. And so her mind had reconstructed the execution scene she'd read about at the photographer's. It was all quite simple and plausible when you thought it through. It had always been easy to sort out her problems here in the cottage. It was healing her now, as she had known it would. Calming her again. Nothing terrible had happened to the people who had lived here in the past. They had led ordinary lives—not too good—not too bad. The smell of the cottage was their smell—a mix of the pleasant and unpleasant—fungus—flowers—sweat—wood-smoke. The cottage sounds were their sounds—laughter—sighs—a little weeping—a little arguing. There had been loving here and tenderness and pain. It was a place of wounds and the healing of wounds. That woman in the photograph had never lived here. Near the village of Mardale, the police report had said. And then London. Not here. Never here. She had nothing to do with the cottage—or her. Ignore her. Forget her.

But she couldn't.

Lowell opened a tin of game soup and heated it. There was enough for two, but he didn't want any. He poured half of it into a mug and took it through. The intruder, meanwhile, had gone to his bedroom, found an old Aran sweater of his, and wrapped herself in it. What was she trying to do, he wondered? Merely keep warm—or establish some sort of link between them—or both? He felt a slight sexual stirring, not strong enough to form a bridge to the near past. She was still a stranger—a girl who had walked in—not someone he had loved with passion and tenderness. Not Rose.

She took the mug from him and cupped her hands around it. The soup smelt appetising and tasted expensive —not starvation rations.

"How are you managing for food?"

"I stocked up when I went home yesterday."

"Did you see your wife?"

A slight hesitation—a glance at the photograph—and then, very casually: "Yes, I saw Zoe."

Your marriage must be your affair, Rose thought, and obviously you're shutting off any discussion about it. Good. Go back to her. Get out of my cottage. Out of my life. She suddenly decided to tell him about Greg, building it up to something more than it was.

He listened in silence, his mind elsewhere. He didn't care who this little whore bedded with. Loved or didn't love. He was remembering Zoe—his hands on her throat. The hard-soft pulsating feel of it. The police would discover her body soon; he had been crazy not to hide it. It was necessary to act while he still had the freedom to act.

Self-preservation had been way down on the list of priorities. It was time to push it up to the top.

Or so the voice in his head was telling him.

He considered possibilities.

There was enough food in the van to keep him going for a while, but not a lot of petrol. There was no point in driving off in it. He wouldn't get far. He would need to protect himself here.

But how?

Rose picked up her mug and took it to be washed. She noticed Middy's dish on the floor and the remains of what looked like tinned salmon on it. Lowell's financial difficulties seemed to be over.

He followed her into the lean-to and she pointed at a tin of shrimps. "For Middy?"

"Yes."

"You're feeding him on the fat of the land."

"I was."

She noticed a listening expression on his face. It was uncanny. She persuaded herself she was imagining it. "What do you mean?"

He didn't answer directly. "Are there foxes around?"

"Yes, occasionally. Why?"

"How are they dealt with? Poison?"

"Of course not. Craddock—the stockman—sees them off with a rifle. He shot a couple last year. They were beautiful animals." She couldn't understand his interest and looked at him anxiously.

"Middy was a beautiful animal." He saw her expression and for a moment the other voice faded out to allow him a few moments of sanity. *Don't hurt her. This girl standing by you is flesh and blood—she's Rose—get out of your pit—reach out to her.*

He put his hand gently on hers, but she took a step backwards and his hand dropped.

"What are you trying to tell me, Lowell?"

With the contact broken, the voice came back strongly. "I found Middy's body this morning. He'd been savaged by a large animal, probably a fox. I need a rifle for a couple of days. Could you get me one from the farm?"

She believed what he was telling her and was deeply grieved. Middy had been there at the beginning of their relationship when the excitement of making love with him was at its peak. The animal's death seemed to underline this parting now. It emphasised the ending.

"I'm sorry." A few weeks ago she would have walked into his arms. Not now.

Last year she had seen the scattered entrails of a young lamb. The memory superimposed on the memory of Middy was sickening. The cat's bloody demise was probably the cause of Lowell's weird behaviour. Shock, anger and booze had blasted reason out of his head.

But Lowell with a gun? He was a musician, not a dealer in death. He couldn't even set up a mousetrap without cutting himself. It seemed wise to dissuade him. "I don't think my grandfather would lend you a rifle—you haven't a licence."

"He needn't know."

No, she thought, he needn't. The rifles weren't under lock and key. It wouldn't be difficult to slip into the farmhouse and get one. But its absence would be noticed soon.

"Would you know how to use it?"

"Yes." There was an edge to his voice. They were wasting time in discussion.

"I don't like killing," she protested, "not even to avenge Middy—even supposing the animal comes again, and it probably won't."

"Do you suppose I like killing?" He was sweating with the effort to keep control. What was she trying to do—force him to stand here and discuss the ethics of it? He had a strong recollection of Zoe sprawled face downwards on the kitchen floor, her fingers touching a pool of acrid-smelling spilt milk.

She shrugged. "All right. If you must. I'll show you where they're kept." After that, she decided, it would be up to him. Whether he returned with a rifle or not, he would return on his own. She wanted no more of him. Here. Anywhere.

She caught a glimpse of her face in the small mirror over the sink. God, she looked frightful! Like a demented squaw! She couldn't go to the farm looking like this.

She poured water from the bucket under the pump into the washing-up bowl and found Lowell's soap, which was of the strong kitchen variety. She soaped her hands and then rubbed her cheeks with them. The water in the bowl turned a deep shade of cinnamon. She poured more, splashed her face, and then, her back to him, asked for the towel.

He didn't move. Everything she did seemed a deliberate act to baulk him. The familiar dreaded thudding inside his head was starting again and the walls were closing in.

She turned in time to see his expression—eyes narrowed—lips tightly compressed. He seemed not to be breathing.

And then he exhaled softly.

The voice was soothing. *Take it gently, Lowell. There's time enough. Walk to the farm with her. Keep calm.*

He handed her a towel and managed to smile. "We'll go and fetch the gun now."

The wind was bending the rough grass on the edges of the path and the sun, obscured intermittently by racing clouds, sent streamers of light over the grey-green of distant meadows. The day, out here, away from the cottage, had the vitality of all things young. A flock of starlings wheeled and plunged and soared and then, banding to-

gether, sped over the field of Charolais cattle like minia-
ture aircraft.

Rose watched Lowell striding ahead of her. Not so long
ago they had strolled along here, side by side, hands
touching. His moments of true tranquillity were rare, but
he'd found them with her. She remembered how he
would sleep briefly after making love and then awaken
slowly and reach out for her to assure himself she was
still there.

Or that other woman was still there.

He had seemed to be communing with the photograph.
Even when he hadn't been looking at it, she had sensed
his awareness of the image. It was more real to him than
she was. She was free of him. It was a good feeling—
wasn't it? He didn't have to be cosseted any more. She
didn't have to watch her language any more. The only
last bizarre thing she had to do for him was to fetch him a
rifle. And she'd back out of that if she could.

She quickened her pace to match his. Why was he
walking so fast? "Lowell, slow down, I can't keep up with
you."

He paused, didn't answer, walked on.

"All right," she snapped, "go. I'm resting."

She went to sit on the wall surrounding the field of
cattle and eased off her shoes. Cheap shoes. Dark green
plastic with high slim heels and silver buckles. Pretty.
How would her grandfather react to her new image, she
wondered? The few days' break away from the farm—
from him—had thrust her into freedom. The groove no
longer held her. More than once in the past he had offered to finance a course of study for her—a finishing
school, he'd suggested—in Switzerland perhaps, or
France. Her thumbs-down now would be less emphatic.
Something—anything different—was worth a try.

She'd miss the cottage, but not the farm.

From this vantage point on the wall she could see the

cottage clearly—brooding, ancient, reassuringly familiar.
It was obvious that at one time it had been part of the
Ballater estate. She had asked her grandfather about its
history, but he had refused to be drawn. No one else
seemed to know—or was reluctant to say. If her grandfather acquired it for road access it would be destroyed.
That mustn't happen. Perhaps, later, when she had her
inheritance, she could outbid him and buy Lowell out.

She saw he was returning to her, his face dark with
anger.

"For God's sake, why are you sitting there?"

"I'm tired. My shoes are making my feet ache."

He glanced at them. They were ridiculous. She was ridiculous. Her crimson blouse was a narrow rim of red
under the Aran sweater where it touched her skimpy
black skirt. Her short stiff hair gleamed garishly in the
sunlight. She looked clownish, even with her face clean.
She was a detestable joke—a caricature of Rose drawn
with venom—a daubing of something beautiful.

Disturbed by his expression, she turned away from him
and looked across the field where the cattle were grazing.
A small black creature was weaving its way through the
grass—a complex pattern of movement—first this way
and then that—a little run forward—a withdrawal—a
slither to the side and a mad dash in a semicircle. A teasing of something. A teasing of the Charolais bull.

From this distance it looked like a small black poodle.
Dogs were brainless enough to bait animals that might
retaliate. It surely must be a dog. A cat would have more
sense.

Rose put her shoes on and stood on a flat piece of stone
at the top of the wall so that she could see more clearly.

It was a cat. Middy.

Delight that the animal was alive was followed by anxiety that it soon wouldn't be. César had lumbered to his

feet, awkwardly, heavily, like a punch-drunk fighter gradually preparing for action.

Lowell had seen Middy, too. Damn him for reappearing at the wrong time! He muttered something about the cat he'd found being badly mauled—he'd thought it was Middy—next time it might be. He still needed the gun.

Rose wasn't listening to him. Middy occasionally behaved wildly in a high wind, but he had never behaved like this before. His antics were extraordinary. The bull was tame enough in normal circumstances, she had always been able to control it, but there were limits to its patience.

It was advancing very slowly with almost comical disbelief towards its tormentor. Middy flashed past its hooves and then, like elastic pulled to full stretch and suddenly released, snapped back in an arc that took him onto the bull's haunches. The cat dug its claws into the flesh under the thick white curls and drew blood.

Rose, unsure what to do, but aware that she must do something before the stupid animal was killed, jumped down into the field. Middy was on the grass again now and running in widening circles around the bull. César watched, moving his great head from side to side.

Rose moved cautiously forward, then crouched, ready to grab the cat on what she estimated would be its return route. It saw her. Swerved. The patterns of circles changed—became a zigzag like flashes of forked lightning—backwards as far as Rose—swiftly forward towards the bull before she could grab it. The zigzags shortened, luring the bull towards her. Twice she almost caught Middy, the cat was tantalisingly close. Next time she'd capture the idiotic creature, get it out of harm's way.

And then it changed direction again, streaking off into the high grass bordering the far hedge.

The bull, intent on something that was no longer there, raised its head and looked for another quarry.

Rose stood still as the bull's eyes locked onto hers.

She had been close to it on other occasions, running her fingers through its hair, grooming it, feeling a degree of affection for it. It had never done her any harm. It surely never would. It needed to be placated. Soothed.

But its eyes now, alert, bloodshot, were menacing, and for the first time she felt a small twist of fear. It was no longer a pet but a creature of immense strength that had been riled. Her César had become unpredictable.

It would be wise to back off. Slowly. All movement would have to be quiet and calm. She took a step backwards. The bull lowered its head, and its right hoof ripped a clod of earth in a neat sharp line. The air smelt pungently of soil and the animal's breath.

She counted five slowly and took another step backwards.

"Stay!" she commanded it softly, scarcely moving her lips.

Another step backwards—and another.

She could hear a distant voice—Craddock's. He understood the animal almost as well as she did. If Lowell went to him for help, she and Craddock could manage the beast between them.

She glanced away from the bull and saw that Lowell was in the field. What the hell did he think he could do here! She wanted to shout at him to get back and fetch Craddock, but couldn't risk raising her voice. In the few seconds she had broken eye contact with the animal she had lost a little dominance over it. If it began moving she would lose all control. It was vital to force her will on it—to hold it hypnotically.

She began to sweat with the effort.

Look at me, César, damn you.

Be still.

Stay . . . Look at me.

Gently, César.

Look at me . . . Here.

Quietly . . . calmly.

Sod you . . . This way . . . Look at me . . . Damn you . . . Look!

She mouthed the jumbled words over and over, suppressing panic. It was looking at Lowell. He was walking towards it. What the fuck did he think he was doing? *Leave César to me. I can handle him. I know him. Clear out of this. Don't interfere.*

He was trying to draw the animal off. Didn't he know he was confusing it more? Didn't he know anything about the nature of the beast?

The bull was beginning to move. Not towards Lowell. Its eyes were locked onto hers again, but this time the hypnotic power was the bull's.

She took several quick steps backwards and the heel of her shoe snapped and threw her off balance. She fell awkwardly and lay rigid with fear in what seemed a forest of rank green weeds that darkened slowly into blackness. She could hear the thudding of hooves and feel the crushing weight of Lowell's body as he flung himself protectively on top of her. The hooves became heartbeats. And then they too were silent.

In the few moments before he died Lowell lay holding her in the pale half-light of a time long ago. She was very small and frail in her nakedness . . . her skin was warm and scented . . . her long, curly, dark hair, thick and beautiful. In the cot beside the bed an infant was mewling softly.

The pain came sharply—a quick thrust between his shoulder blades—a piercing of his lung. The lace-edged pillow was getting spattered with blood—and so were her face and hair. She was looking up at him—or at the other one behind him—her eyes a blind expressionless blue. He couldn't read them. Was too mortally hurt to try. He wanted to kiss her, but there was blood in his mouth. It tasted of salt. Like tears.

He loved her, and their child, more than he had ever loved anyone in his life. And tried to keep holding her. But she was pushing him away.

EPILOGUE

The coroner's court was well attended for the inquest.
The death of a once-famous musician in unusual circumstances was widely reported on the second page of most
of the dailies. A professor of music, an ex-colleague of
Lowell's, paid tribute to him in the obituary column of
the *Daily Telegraph*. The possibility of a memorial service
was mooted.

All things considered, Zoe decided, she had been wise
to come. She wore her mink coat. A Dior scarf in shades
of purple and grey was carefully arranged around her
neck, disguising the heavy bruising. Dark glasses camou-
flaged her emotions. The widow must appear to grieve.

That it might easily have been a double inquest, had
Lowell's hands been less distorted and more capable of
exerting sufficient pressure, was a fact that must never be
publicised. Had he been less drunk, he might have realised she wasn't dead, and finished her off some other
way. Equally, had he been sober, it might not have happened at all. It was better not to know.

It was fortuitous that Ben had found her in time. He
had heard the van leaving, he explained to her afterwards, and had called to invite her round for a bite of
supper—a drink—companionship. Lights had been blazing everywhere, and the back door was open. He had

tactfully said as little as possible about finding her semi-
conscious—and resuscitating her—but his shock and anger were obvious. When, some while later, she was capable of speaking—painfully and not very coherently—she
had stopped his phoning the police. This was a family
matter, she'd insisted. Lowell's uncle, Sir Howard, must
be told. But no one else. Lowell might have to be committed to a psychiatric hospital. If so, the less said the better.
That family shame should be averted quite so dramati-
cally was a welcome reprieve. She was wise enough not to
say so.

Ben, seated beside her, was watching her anxiously. He
had tried to dissuade her from attending the inquest—she
wasn't needed here and had surely been too hurt physically and emotionally to bear much more. But she seemed
surprisingly calm. Never at any stage of recovery had she
cried. Louise's reaction had been far more emotional. A
friend had died and she mourned him. His assault on Zoe
was horrendous, she said, but he wasn't altogether to
blame. "He crept into that cottage like a hermit crab—
because he was unhappy at home. If he hadn't gone there
—gone somewhere else—he would have been all right.
That horrible dump did something to him."

Ben had pointed out that Lowell's mental breakdown
was due to a variety of factors which built up stress—not
just the environment. The catalyst was the girl. The one
he'd ranted about to Zoe. The one who'd made a hero of
him. Rose. The exquisite irony wasn't lost on him. He
was curious to hear her evidence, and wondered how Zoe
would react. But first it was the stockman's turn to go on
the witness stand.

Craddock, looking and feeling uncomfortable in an ill-
fitting navy blue suit, spoke tersely. The cat had unearthed a wasps' nest and been stung. Badly. It had run
wild for a bit around the bull. Upsetting it. Miss Ballater
should have left both animals alone. Not safe to interfere.

Mr. Marshall had tried to push Miss Ballater clear when the bull charged. Not enough time. Got himself killed.

He blew his nose on his khaki handkerchief, returned it to his pocket and waited stiffly for further interrogation.

The coroner, a mild little man with faded blue eyes and sandy hair, had farming connections. A bull the size and weight of the Charolais tended to use its muscles rather than its horns. In this case, the horn thrust had been as sharp as a dagger. And it hadn't followed up with any rough stuff—no crushing—no tossing—it had just backed off. According to the autopsy report, however, there was no doubt whatsoever that Marshall's lung had been pierced by the horn.

He asked the stockman if there was anything else he would like to say, as the only near witness of the attack.

There was a lot Craddock could have said, but out of respect for Colonel Ballater it was better to remain silent. It was gossip, of course. Old wives' tales. The coroner would tell him he was talking through his hat—as he himself had told the villagers when he'd had a pint with them in the pub the other evening. Anne-Marie walked, they said, on the anniversary of her execution. It was a time of violence. Too many tragedies, like the killing of the musician, had happened in the village on that date for it to be coincidence. She had been convicted on circumstantial evidence. Perhaps wrongly. Innocent blood sought the blood of the innocent.

Craddock had heard similar stories from Miss Marshall when he had bought herbal cures for his warts from her many years ago.

Anne-Marie Ballater might have made a bad match when she married Tarrant, a farm labourer, she told him, but during the time she had lived in the cottage with him and their little daughter she had been happy. It had been a happy place.

So why had she left them both and bedded down with

her lover in London? Craddock had sneered. Could Miss Marshall's crystal ball tell him that?

If she had been annoyed by his scepticism she hadn't shown it. But she hadn't answered him, either. How could she? Instead she had nattered on about the dead returning to places of great pain—or of great happiness. Those with psychic powers—and some children—knew that. There was no feeling of great pain here, she had insisted. Or of evil. Despite what some of the villagers said. The cottage was peaceful. Safe. A good place to be.

And then she had spoken of Rose. The little girl liked visiting. When she watched her playing around the cottage, she sensed the other one's presence. There was a blood link. She had told the child nothing, of course. The child herself seemed unaware.

The coroner was still waiting for an answer. "Have you anything else to tell us that's relevant, Mr. Craddock?"

Craddock looked across the court to where the Colonel was sitting. Their eyes met briefly. He turned back to the coroner and shook his head. "No, sir," he said.

His stockman had acquitted himself very well, Ballater thought. He hadn't said too much. He hoped his granddaughter would behave with equal good sense. Her appearance, at least, couldn't be faulted. She had washed the muck out of her hair and was appropriately dressed. The tweed suit would, he was sure, be discarded after today for something more garish. A costly waste, but no matter. She was speaking the oath in a low clear voice. He listened uneasily. Rose's truth was many-faceted.

Zoe, expecting Lowell's whore to look quite different, was surprised to see a young girl—a teenager—with short neat hair, no make-up, and wearing a jacket and matching skirt in a quiet shade of blue. A country girl. An innocent. Respectable. Surely not the girl in the photograph whose eyes she had carefully torn into shreds . . . the girl who owned the Victorian dress that Lowell had gone demented over . . . the girl who had wrecked the marriage. The image of Lowell's weakness—the other woman's strength—faded. It couldn't have been like that. Lowell surely was the seducer—if this were the girl. Hatred against the unknown Rose that had been building up like water against a dam began oozing away. She felt cheated. It was necessary to hate. She touched the scarf around her throat and it loosened slightly. She coughed and felt pain. For the first time since Lowell's death she was close to tears. It was unbelievable that Lowell should have tried to kill her on account of the girl over there.

The more Zoe listened to Rose's evidence the more unbelievable it became.

Mr. Marshall owned the cottage near her grandfather's farm, Rose told the coroner. She had seen him coming and going. There was a right-of-way across the farm land which the musician sometimes used. She had been walking home across the field where the Charolais cattle were when the bull got nasty. Mr. Marshall had been on the other side of the wall. He had noticed and come to her aid. So had the stockman and two of the other farmhands, but by the time they were in the field Mr. Marshall had been gored. It had been courageous of him to shield her like that. It was a debt she could never repay.

The debt she could never repay was a well-rehearsed cliché. The debt, if it had ever existed, was being repaid now. Her grandfather hadn't briefed her—exactly—but he had warned her that other people, not just herself, could be hurt. Be circumspect, he had said.

She was being *very* circumspect. It was tempting to stop. To hurl a bomb at everyone's complacency. She looked around the court. Apart from her grandfather and Craddock she didn't know anyone. Lots of curious faces. One woman muffled in mink. Odd way of finding entertainment on a warm autumn day. It would be amusing to make the entertainment really sizz. We went to bed, she'd tell them, Lowell and I. He was a fantastic lay. But in the end he was crazy. Tried to trick me into getting a gun. Who do you suppose he wanted to shoot? His wife, perhaps? Or me? As for all that heroic stuff—don't kid yourselves about that. He tripped and fell on top of me when César charged . . . Well, that was the way it had seemed. Though in the few moments of darkness it could have been otherwise. *And they had loved once.*

The coroner told her with kindly concern that the musician's death mustn't trouble her conscience. He had acted voluntarily. No blame attached to her.

No blame about anything, she thought. The abortion four years ago had been necessary after first-time sex with a boy she hardly knew. Necessary—but at fourteen a bit of a shock. She'd had an emotional hang-up about it. And that was what it was all about, wasn't it? Well, wasn't it? Lowell with his weird ways had opened a dark door in her mind and made her see ordinary things darkly—differently. His death had closed it again. All right. Fine. Finished. All is normal.

The verdict was death by misadventure. Rose, unstirred by ancient memories, ancient terrors, of Anne-Marie, smiled as she heard it. Very soon now she would walk out into the sunlight of a lovely autumn afternoon. Young. Free. With all the years ahead of her and glad to be alive. What more could anyone want?

B. M. Gill is one of Britain's premier crime novelists. She has won a Crime Writers' Association Gold Dagger Award and has been twice nominated for the Mystery Writers of America Edgar Award—a rare tribute for a British author. She lives in Anglesey, Wales.